invitation
only

ALSO BY
KATE BRIAN

PRIVATE

The Princess and the Pauper
Lucky T
The V Club
Sweet 16

invitation only

KATE BRIAN

SIMON AND SCHUSTER

SIMON & SCHUSTER
First published in Great Britain in 2007 by Simon & Schuster UK Ltd,
Africa House, 64–78 Kingsway, London WC2B 6AH
A CBS COMPANY

Originally published in the USA in 2006 by Simon Pulse,
an imprint of Simon & Schuster Children's Division, New York.

  Produced by Alloy Entertainment
151 West 26th Street, New York, NY 10001

A CIP catalogue record for this book is
available from the British Liabrary

ISBN-10: 1-41693-244-5
ISBN-13: 978-1-41693-244-4

10 9 8 7 6 5 4 3 2 1

This book is a work of fiction. Names, characters, places and
incidents are either a product of the author's imagination or are
used fictitiously. Any resemblance to actual people living or dead,
events or locales is entirely coincidental.

Printed and bound in Great Britain by
Cox & Wyman, Reading, Berkshire

K.B. would like to thank the following members

of the circle for their support . . .

At A.E.: L.W., J.B., L.M., B.S., M.F., R.D.

At S.P.(et al): E.M., A.B., S.W., J.Z., C.B.

And, as always: M.V.

whittaker

It was a cold night. Cold and extremely dark, with no stars and no moon and a wind that ripped a deluge of leaves from the trees whenever it blew—leaves that were still wet from a morning drizzle. They felt slimy and foul when they happened to fall on exposed skin, so as another gust whipped through the hills, we all ducked and covered. I felt myself begin to shiver.

"Augh! There's one on my neck!" Taylor Bell cried, doubling over with her shoulders to her ears. She clutched the bottle of vodka she'd been swigging from all night in one hand and slapped ineffectively at her back with the other. The large yellow maple leaf had sucked itself almost all the way around her neck, matting down the blond curls that had escaped from the back of her ponytail. "Get it off!"

Normally, Taylor was not the biggest drinker, but tonight she had been pounding straight alcohol like it was the nectar of the gods, perhaps because she, like many others, felt the need to expunge parents weekend—which had ended just hours ago with a ceremony in the Easton Academy chapel—from her memory. Taylor's parents had seemed like nice people, though, and she had appeared to be at least comfortable in their presence. I wondered if something else could be bothering her.

"Get it off!" she whimpered again. "Guys!"

"Don't look at me," Kiran Hayes said, taking a ladylike swig from her silver flask. She pulled her long cashmere coat around her knees and held it there. "I just had a paraffin wrap."

Kiran, the first actual model I had ever known and one of the more gorgeous girls I had ever seen in real life, had always just had *something* done. Highlights, lowlights, dermabrasion, seaweed thigh wrap, eyebrow threading. Most of it sounded like torture, but apparently it all worked.

Noelle Lange rolled her eyes and plucked the large wet leaf from Taylor's skin. "Prima donnas," she said derisively. She whipped the leaf at the ground, and it landed right in front of the long, flat rock on which Ariana Osgood sat. Ariana looked down at the leaf for a moment, studying it as if it held the meaning of life. A lighter breeze lifted her long, almost white-blond hair from her shoulders and she looked up into it, then closed her eyes in pleasure.

I pulled my third beer from the cooler across the clearing and watched this tableau unfold like I was an anthropologist studying some previously unclassified subset of human. I had been fascinated with the Billings Girls from the moment I had first seen them a month ago through the window of my sophomore dorm at

Easton Academy—fascinated from afar, that is, with seemingly no hope of ever gaining up-close access. But that hadn't been the case for long. The Billings Girls were now my friends. My dorm mates. The people with whom I partied illegally in the woods on the outskirts of campus on a regular basis.

If you could call "twice" a regular basis.

I was one of them now. I had ascended to greatness at Easton. Though if someone asked me to sit down and tell them how I had done it, I would be rendered speechless. Last I checked, I had pissed them all off by continuing to talk to my boyfriend, Thomas Pearson, of whom none of them approved. I thought I had lost them forever by going behind their backs and offering to stick with him and help him through his issues. Instead, I had apparently impressed them.

Somehow. And thank God I had, because with their help I might actually have a shot of leaving my past behind. Of not being one of the many Croton, PA, progeny who return to the hometown after two years of community college to take assistant management positions at Costco. With the Billings Girls behind me, I actually had a shot at a life. A future. A shot at being part of a world I had only ever dreamed of—a world of success. Of privilege. Of freedom.

"Are you all right over there, Reed?" Noelle asked, lifting her long, dark hair over her shoulder. "If you don't want another beer I'm sure Kiran would be happy to mix up a Hayes Special for you."

Her eyes danced with mischief and I knew she had noticed my

state of contemplation. I didn't want to appear ungrateful for having been invited here, for everything they had done for me. For the fact that I was getting a beer for myself, rather than running errands for them, as I had been doing pretty much nonstop since the first week of school. So I waved her off.

"That's okay. I'm good with this," I said, lifting the bottle.

I used the rusted bottle opener to pop the cap off and took a long drink, knowing she was still watching me. Earlier tonight I had my first beer ever. Now I was on my third one, which was going down more smoothly. The key, it seemed, was to take long drinks and not let it stay in my mouth long enough to touch my tongue. Yeah. Refreshing. I took a deep breath and let it out into another cold breeze, pulling my sweater closer to my goose-bumped skin. I was about to rejoin the girls, when a sudden conversation shift near the fire stopped me.

"I'll tell you one thing," Dash McCafferty said. "This is going to go down as one of the great disappearing acts of all time."

"Maybe he's at his grandmother's in Boston," Josh Hollis suggested.

Dash shrugged. "Eh, I'm sure they already raided the old bat's place."

Thomas. They were talking about Thomas. I couldn't believe that the last time I was here, he was here as well. It had been approximately forty-eight hours since anyone had seen Thomas Pearson. He had disappeared from Easton without leaving so much as a note behind. And, according to his roommate Josh

Hollis—who stood near the fire with the other guys just then, staring into the flames—Thomas had gone without packing one stitch of clothing, not even his favorite black T-shirt. On Friday morning Thomas had told me he loved me, had made me promise I would be there for him no matter what, and had then proceeded to vanish.

I wondered how much Josh knew—about me, about what Thomas and I had done together. Had Thomas *told* Josh what we had done in their dorm room? I wasn't sure. I hadn't known him long enough to find out. But now, every time I saw Josh, I wondered if he knew what I'd done and the thought made me squirm. I didn't need half the school knowing I had lost my virginity to a guy who maybe meant well but was clearly too troubled to be in a healthy relationship. Lost my virginity to a guy who I now knew (even before he vanished) I probably should not be with, but who I still felt irresistably attached to anyway. Lost my virginity to Thomas Pearson, the most popular guy at Easton and also, as I'd recently discovered, the campus's foremost drug supplier. I still couldn't believe it.

Josh took a swig of his previously untouched beer. He had such a baby face that he looked out of place holding the green glass bottle. His blond curls danced in the breeze and he wore a long, striped scarf over a wrinkly, rust-colored T-shirt and brown corduroy jacket. He had that artsy, earnest, creative thing going. I liked that about him. I also liked the fact that he had a loud voice— loud enough for me to eavesdrop without letting on.

"What about their place in Vail?" he offered.

"Dude, Pearson is not holing up anywhere obvious. Believe me," Dash said with an elaborate snarfle of phlegm. For an extraordinarily good-looking guy—chiseled, blond, Abercrombie-esque—he had some serious hygiene flaws. He spat into the fire and took a swig of his beer.

"Very attractive, Dash," Noelle called across the clearing.

"Thanks, babe," he replied, and then got back to the topic at hand. "I just can't believe they called the local police in. It's such a waste. If Pearson is crashing anywhere, he's crashing in New York."

"You think?" The hope in Josh's voice gave life to my own.

"Are you kidding?" Gage Coolidge said. Gage was of the skinny, tall, metrosexual variety, with dark hair that stood straight up from his head—he looked like a member of some British pretty-boy band. "Thomas Pearson is pulling the biggest punk of all time right now. He's got the entire eastern seaboard looking for him and he's off somewhere partying himself sick."

"Yeah, maybe," Josh said, chewing on his inner cheek and staring at the fire.

"No maybe," Dash told him. "Trust me. Halloween is in less than a month. And you know what that means."

"The Legacy," Josh said.

"Exactly." Dash removed one finger from his beer bottle and pointed it at Josh. "Pearson is not going to miss that. If his ass isn't there, I'll give up the Lotus."

"That's serious, man," Gage said.

"No shit."

"It's true," Josh said, nodding. "Pearson *is* the Legacy."

"Dude. If he's there, we should drag his sorry ass back up here and collect our medals," Gage said.

"Aw, yeah," Dash replied, smacking hands with Gage over Josh's head.

The Legacy? What the heck was the Legacy? I pushed myself away from the tree where I had been lounging, figuring Noelle and the others could clue me in, but before I could take a step, Natasha Crenshaw intercepted me.

"Reed! Where are you going?" she asked, slinging her arm around my neck.

I froze, wondering what the joke was. Natasha Crenshaw was my new roommate at Billings House. And the only reason she was my new roommate was because her best friend, Leanne Shore, had gotten kicked out for cheating in the biggest public scandal Easton had seen all year. Ever since I'd started to unpack my stuff yesterday morning, Natasha had been seething with resentment. It dripped from her very pores.

Thus my current state of confusion.

"You okay?" I asked her.

"I'm fine!" she said, her pearly whites nearly blinding me. Natasha was dark-skinned, dark-haired, and Tyra Banks bodacious. I could feel all the soft curves of her body as she pressed it closer to mine and it made me blush. As a woman of seriously boy-like proportions, I had no idea how she walked around with all that stuff. "Listen. I just wanted to apologize if I've been less than welcoming the last couple of days," she said, pulling me back away from the guys. "I'm still a little upset about Leanne and I think I've been taking it out on you. And that's not cool. Do you forgive me?"

The other thing about Natasha was that she was always coming out with these frank, no-nonsense statements. Unlike every other girl I had ever known, she seemed to have nothing to hide. It was a foreign concept.

"Uh . . . sure," I said uncertainly.

"Good! Because I really want us to be friends," Natasha said, grasping my hand. "Good friends."

Her expression was so earnest it made me smile, half in amusement, half in genuine pleasure.

"Okay. I'd like that too," I said.

"Good!" Natasha cried. She produced a miniscule digital camera from the pocket of her black leather jacket and held it up with one hand, while hugging me to her with her other. "Smile!"

I did as told and the flash went off. I blinked at the floating purple spots.

"An instant classic," Natasha declared, checking the tiny screen.

"Cool." I glanced past her at Josh and the others, who were now conferencing in lower voices. I wondered if they were still talking about Thomas, and if they would tell me anything if they were. "I'll . . . be right back."

I was halfway across to the fire when suddenly all the guys looked up as one and shouted, right at me, "Whittaker!"

I nearly tripped. "What?"

"Gentlemen! Ladies! Ah, it warms my heart to see everyone gathered here, just like old times."

Huh?

Walking up behind me was the largest specimen of a guy I had ever seen outside a college football game. He had to be at least six foot four and was well over 250 pounds, but he carried all that weight with dignity, his shoulders back, his stride confident. He had ruddy cheeks, round glasses, and a much older man's haircut, the kind that stood up in the front about an inch and was matted down with gel in the back. He strode across the clearing, nodding to the Billings Girls like some aristocrat before reaching out a hand to smack palms with Dash, Gage, Josh, and the others.

"How are we all this fine evening?" he asked in his booming voice. He placed his hands over the fire, rubbed them together, and then held them out again.

Who *was* this guy? And why did he talk like he'd just stepped out of a Jane Austen novel?

"How was East Asia? Is Chinese food really better in China?" Gage joked, swigging his beer.

I missed Whittaker's response due to another gust of wind, but all the guys laughed at whatever he had to say, gathering around and looking up at him with amused smiles and excited eyes. It was as if Santa Claus had just walked into a room full of kindergarteners. I found myself gravitating slowly toward Noelle and the others.

"Reed, I was starting to think you'd forgotten about us," Noelle said flatly, taking a sip of her beer. She was the only Billings Girl who drank beer, which had been my motivation in choosing it. The rest opted for mixed drinks made from whatever bottles Kiran and the boys managed to procure. "What're you, in love all over again?"

"Huh?"

"You can't stop staring at Whittaker," Kiran put in, her brown eyes gleaming. "Interesting choice."

"Please. I'm not staring," I said. "I'm just . . . Who is he?"

"Whittaker?" Noelle said. "He's . . . Whittaker. He is a class unto himself." She looked around at the other Billings Girls and slowly smiled. "In fact . . . you should meet him."

She got up, grabbed my wrist, and started pulling me across the clearing, all in one motion—all before I could get out a word of protest.

"Whit! Hey, Whit!" Noelle shouted, gesturing with her bottle. "This is the girl I was telling you about."

She used her tremendous arm strength to practically whip me at Whittaker. The sudden velocity took me by surprise and I stumbled, bracing my hands against his large chest to stop my fall. All the guys, of course, cracked up laughing. Whittaker put his hands gently on my elbows and steadied me.

"Are you all right?" he asked.

He had very warm brown eyes.

"Fine," I said, embarrassed.

Wait a second. Had Noelle said I was the girl she had *told* him about? What the hell had she been saying?

"I'm Walt Whittaker," he said, offering his hand. "But my friends call me Whittaker or Whit. Your preference."

"Reed Brennan," I said, shaking his hand. It was unbelievably soft and warm.

"So, Reed. You're new to Easton, I understand. Welcome," he said.

The timbre of his voice made my skin tingle in a pleasing, humming way. It was comforting. Familiar, somehow.

"You're not?" I asked.

Again, everyone laughed. Even Whit. "No. No. My family has been a fixture here for generations," he said. "I've just been on holiday with my parents. We did a tour of East Asia. China, Singapore, Hong Kong, the Philippines. . . . Do you travel, Reed?"

Not unless you count all those trips to Hershey Park back when I still wore pink sneakers.

"Not really," I said.

He looked at me for a long moment, as if what I had just said did not compute. I started to grow warm under his scrutiny,

"That's a shame," he said finally. "You can't truly know yourself until you've seen the world, you know?"

I was struggling to formulate an answer that wouldn't make me sound naïve and unworldly when Gage slapped his hand down on Whittaker's shoulder from behind.

"Dude! Get over here! We were just talking about the Legacy. You gotta tell us what you know."

Whittaker smirked. "Ah, the Legacy. So it begins," he said.

What *was* this Legacy thing? I wanted to ask, but it seemed like one of those things that all of them already knew about, so if I asked about it, I would just be making it abundantly clear that *I* knew nothing—thereby reminding them of what an outsider I was. I decided to keep my mouth shut and hope I'd be able to overhear all about it in time.

"Perhaps we can catch up later?" he said to me.

"Uh . . . sure," I replied.

Gage pulled Whittaker off for a private confab with the boys and Noelle stepped up next to me.

"So? Work your spell on him yet?" Noelle asked.

"You *told* him about me?" I said.

"Yeah. I thought maybe you guys could get to know each other," Noelle said with a shrug. "Whit could be good for you. He's very . . . cultured."

I ignored the implied insult in that statement.

"Noelle! I'm with Thomas, remember?" I said. I no longer cared that she didn't want me to be with Thomas. The fact that he had mysteriously disappeared kind of negated all other concerns.

Her expression turned hard. "Right. And Thomas is . . . where?" she asked, looking around.

"I . . . I don't know," I said, my stomach responding with a clench. Over her shoulder, I watched Ariana, Kiran, and Taylor approaching, clearly interested in the topic of our private tête-à-tête.

"Exactly. Some boyfriend, bailing and not even telling you where he's going. Or *that* he's going," she said. She rolled her eyes again and took another sip of beer, allowing this to sink in. "Look, Whit is a great guy. He's a *nice* guy."

"Unlike some people," Kiran said snarkily.

Even with his mysterious disappearance they couldn't let their disdain for Thomas go. They had never liked him. They never would.

"Plus, Whit can give you things," Ariana put in. "Things you might not otherwise have access to."

Give me things, huh? Well, color me curious.

Ariana gazed at Whit with her clear blue eyes and I wondered if he felt it. If it gave him the chills the way it always did me.

"Like what?" I said.

"Like a life," Kiran said with a snort.

"Kiran!" Ariana scolded.

"Just go talk to him," Noelle said. "You don't have to marry the guy."

I took a deep breath and drained the last dregs of my beer, all the while keeping an eye on Whit. He seemed nice. Polite and mature. Plus the guys clearly loved him. And yeah, maybe he was a little overweight, but who was I to judge?

"Bring him some of this," Kiran said, handing over a spare flask of her Hayes Special. "Whittaker loves my recipes."

The flask was ice cold and sleek to the touch. I held it in one hand, my beer in the other. Maybe it was time to give a Billings-sanctioned guy a chance. After all, I was a Billings Girl now too. It seemed high time I started acting like one.

something to impress

"It was eye opening, I have to say, living among the locals," Whittaker said as we strolled away from the clearing. "They have nothing. Nothing but a wooden bowl and a cup of rice to eat, but they have spirit, you know? Such spirit."

"So you slept in the village?" I asked, keeping my eyes trained on my feet. I was on the fourth beer now, and things were starting to get the slightest bit bleary. "That's so cool."

I couldn't remember whose idea it had been for us to go off alone and get to know each other. His? Mine? Noelle's?

"Oh, no. We went back to the hotel, of course," Whit said. "Do you realize the number of diseases one can pick up in a place like that?"

I looked up waiting for him to acknowledge the irony. "But I thought you said you lived among them." Just then, my foot hit a rock and slid, twisting my ankle inward. I stumbled and fell sideways into Whittaker. "Oh. Whoops!"

"Are you quite well?" he asked me, using both meaty arms to steady me.

I cleared my throat. Around me the trees tilted and swayed. "Yes. Quite," I said, mimicking his tone. Who talked like this?

"Perhaps we should sit," he suggested.

Now the ground tilted. Why did anyone ever say drinking was fun? This was actually quite nauseating. "Yes. Perhaps we should."

Whittaker led me over to a thick log that had fallen sometime in the past century and was now overgrown with moss and vines. He lowered me down slowly until I was steadily seated, and only then did he let me go. I braced one hand on the cold, rough wood to keep from falling over and shook my hair back. Whittaker smiled as he sat next to me, studying my face.

"Noelle didn't lie. You really are quite beautiful," he said. "You have a classic look about you. Like Grace Kelly."

"Grace who?" I asked.

Whittaker's smile widened slightly. "She was an actress. And a princess. Actually, it was quite an incredible story. She started out as a poor farm girl, then became hugely famous in Hollywood, married a European prince—"

"Sounds good to me," I said blearily, lifting my beer bottle in a toast.

"Then died in a fiery car crash," Whittaker finished.

"Oh." Nice. Thanks a lot.

Whittaker suddenly flushed and looked away, taking a drink from his flask. "Would you like some?" he asked.

Somewhere in my brain I knew it probably wasn't a good idea

to drink anything else, but I also knew that Kiran mixed some kind of juice into her special concoction. And somewhere else in my brain, something decided that it might be a good idea to consume juice. Since it had vitamins and all.

"Sure," I said. "Why not?"

I placed my nearly empty beer bottle down on the ground and almost fell over. My palm hit the dirt and I pushed myself back up, trying to cover, but my equilibrium was shot. When I reached for the flask, I tipped over into Whittaker's arms. My eyes closed in embarrassment and the ground shifted. Great. Now my brain was totally misfiring.

"Sorry," I said.

"That's all right," he replied. "Here. Let me help."

He placed one of his solid arms around me and I instantly felt more secure, less wobbly. I managed to get the top off the flask and took a long drink. Mmmmm. The Hayes Special was yummy. And Whittaker was so warm. I closed my eyes, savoring the moment, and tipped the flask back. Once again the ground shifted. I jerked and the liquid went down the wrong pipe. All airways closed off and I choked, spitting alcohol everywhere.

"Are you all right?" Whittaker asked.

"Fine! Fine!" I choked, doubling over. Whittaker fished out a handkerchief from his pocket and handed it to me. I coughed into it and wiped my face. The handkerchief was soft, smelled of musk, and had his initials embroidered into it. Old school all the way. No one I knew even owned handkerchiefs, but somehow I was not surprised.

"I'm so sorry," I said, finally catching my breath. I tried to hand the handkerchief back to him, but he closed his hand over mine, which closed over the cloth.

"Keep it. It's yours," he said.

I flushed. "You must think I'm a total loser," I said.

"Quite the contrary," he said, looking into my eyes. "I think you're extraordinary."

And then he was kissing me. Okay. Not good! I was not supposed to be kissing Walt Whittaker. I was supposed to be kissing Thomas. Thomas, my boyfriend. Thomas, the perfectly gorgeous guy who had taken my virginity. If only he were here. If only I knew where the hell he was.

Thoughts of Thomas flooded my mind. Thomas, Thomas, Thomas. Thomas's lips, Thomas's hands, Thomas's fingers, Thomas's tongue . . .

And suddenly, I *was* kissing him. His sweet, warm mouth; his strong, lean arms. Even with everything we had gone through in the past few days, I missed his touch. That was the one thing with Thomas that was *never* wrong.

Half delirious, I slipped my hands around Whit's thick neck. The second I did he got confident. His mouth moved over mine in a rough, unpracticed, awkward back-and-forth motion, so fast it was as if he was trying to create fire with our lips.

Ugh. Very *not* Thomas. I grabbed his face between both my

hands to stop the madness and he took it as a sign of enthusiasm. Suddenly his tongue was everywhere, parting my lips and darting between my teeth.

This poor kid. He had no idea what he was doing. I wanted to push him away, but I didn't want to embarrass him. Instead I let him go and hoped he would either suddenly improve or get winded and stop.

Then his large hand fell right on top of my breast and squeezed. Hard. Like he was juicing an orange.

Just like that, Thomas was back. Right there in front of me. With his sexy smile and his practiced, gentle touch and his skin against mine. What the hell was I doing? Who *was* this person who was groping me like I was some kind of CPR doll?

My stomach lurched. I held my breath. Oh, God. I was going to throw up. I was going to barf in Walt Whittaker's mouth.

My hands flew up and I shoved him away from me. He was just letting out a confused murmur when I turned around, keeled over, and retched all over the bed of leaves behind the log. My eyes stung; my throat burned; my stomach wrenched in pain. Whittaker stood up and moved away, turning his back to me to give me privacy. Thank God. The last thing I wanted was for the guy I had just kissed to watch me puke all over the place.

And then, finally, it was over.

"Are you all right?" Whittaker asked me.

It was like his refrain of the evening.

I nodded slowly, too mortified to speak.

"Can I walk you back to Billings?" he asked.

I nodded again. Whittaker held out his hands and helped me up. He wrapped his arm around me as we walked back to the clearing and I leaned in to him, mushy as overcooked pasta. Everyone stared at our arrival. I could only imagine what I looked like. For a fleeting moment my unfocused gaze fell on Josh. He looked as grim as death.

"Aw! Look at you two, all coupley," Noelle said with a knowing smile.

I watched as Josh quickly looked away, swigging his beer.

"I'm going to walk her back," Whittaker announced, sounding proud.

"Nice," Dash said under his breath.

"Take care of our girl," Noelle said, patting Whit on the back.

From somewhere deep inside of me, I summoned a trace of a smile. Even in my extraordinary state of queasy shame, I felt the warmth of Noelle's approval. And though I knew it was totally spineless to bask in it, I did. Noelle's approval was always a good thing.

cinderella lives

The first thing I recognized was the dirty gutter taste in my dry-as-talc mouth. The second was the blinding pain in my skull. The third was the fact that I was freezing. The fourth was the banging.

The banging. The banging. The incessant banging.

"Wake up, new girl! It's after six! You're never going to get anywhere with this attitude!"

Each bang reverberated in my skull and shot a new stab of pain through my head.

I wrenched my eyes open, then blinked a couple hundred times against their painful dryness. In front of me was the cream-colored wall of my dorm. Below me was my mattress. Nothing else was right.

"That's right, sleepyhead. Vacation's over! Get your sorry ass out of bed!"

It was Noelle. Noelle was yelling over the banging. I flipped over onto my back, the pain in my head nearly blinding, and looked up. I had to swallow back a sudden influx of bile in my throat. Not just Noelle: Kiran, Taylor, Ariana, Natasha, and four other Billings Girls whose names I couldn't remember in my current state of excruciating pain hovered over me. Kiran was pounding a red and black steel drum with the handle end of a pair of scissors. Noelle had folded something white and ruffly over her arm. Taylor held a DustBuster with grim determination, her eyes hollow and rimmed with hangover red. Natasha gripped my covers in her hands at the end of my bed—thus the goose bumps and shivers.

"What the hell are you guys doing?" I whimpered, squeezing my eyes closed. The banging, mercifully, had stopped. I pressed both palms into my forehead to keep my brain from gouging its way out.

"It's chore time, new girl," Noelle said.

As my brow screwed up in confusion, I felt another shock wave of pain through my temples. "What?"

She grabbed both my wrists and yanked me up into a seated position. My head exploded and I was seized by an overwhelming urge to heave. As I gasped for breath, sweating and praying that I wouldn't puke in front of everyone, Noelle slipped her frilly something over my head, then tied it behind my back. When I was able to open my eyes again, I was wearing a white French maid–style apron over my pajamas. Pinned to the left strap was a big red button that read NEED HELP? JUST ASK! MY NAME IS GLASS-LICKER.

I groaned. It was about all I could summon the energy to do.

"You didn't think you were done, did you?" Kiran asked. Her highlighted hair was piled atop her head and her dark skin shone against the white silk of her robe as if it had been polished. The girl had imbibed more than anyone last night and yet this morning she looked gorgeous enough to be photographed. "No, no, no, no, no. Why did you think we let you *in* here? Now we have access to you twenty-four seven. And that means that you get to do whatever we ask you to do twenty-four seven. That *is* how it works, isn't it?" she asked with mock seriousness, looking around at her friends.

"Well, yes. I believe it is," Ariana said, her light southern accent softening the betrayal of her words.

They had to be kidding me. They were really going to drag me out of bed in the middle of my first hangover to work? After everything I had done for them just to get in here, there was still more? I had thought this proving-myself thing was over. That I was officially one of them. Apparently the torture was just beginning.

Suddenly I felt hollow inside, which, on top of the excruciating head pain and the gut-clenching nausea, was not fun. But what was I going to do? Say no? Yeah, right. I'd be back in Bradwell and at Sophomore-Nothing status before you could say, "Suck it."

"Here," Taylor said, shoving the DustBuster at me. Her hangover had aged her normally nubile and chipper self at least ten years. "I haven't dusted under my bed since I've been here. It's starting to affect my sinuses."

Dumbly, I took the contraption from her and held it against my chest, petrified of what might happen if I moved again. The detachment of my head from my body seemed likely.

"And when you're done with that you can make all the beds," Noelle said. "And vacuum the halls before breakfast. The real vacuum is in the hall supply closet."

I stared up at them, my temples throbbing, hoping they would all laugh and tell me it was just a joke. They gazed back at me with impatience.

"You're serious," I croaked.

Noelle scrunched her nose, waving her hand in front of it. "I suggest you Listerine first," she said. "I don't want your toxic breath stinking up my room."

"Glass-licker, huh? Still?" one of the nameless girls asked, tilting her head. "Don't you think we should change the nickname to something more apropos? Like Glass-cleaner?"

"Or Glass-scrubber," Taylor suggested.

"Glass-wiper?" Natasha added.

Noelle narrowed her eyes, considering. "Nah. They just don't have the same ring. She's Glass-licker all the way."

I flinched as she patted my shoulder. Hard.

"Let's go, ladies," Noelle sang.

Together they all traipsed out. Everyone but Natasha, who dropped my sheets on the floor and stepped on them with her bare feet on her way to our shared bathroom. I wanted to get up. I did. But between the pain in my skull, the churning in my belly, and the dryness in my throat, it didn't seem physically possible.

"Oh, and if you don't get it all done before breakfast, you'll be taking a toothbrush to the toilets tonight," Noelle said, pausing by the door. "*Your* toothbrush."

"I'm up!" I said, standing straight. Instantly the entire room caved in around me, crushing my cranium. I closed my eyes against a new wave of nausea.

"That's my girl," Noelle said.

Then she made a point of slamming the door.

inside the inside

"I like my pillows fluffed," Cheyenne Martin told me as she pinned her diamond studs through her ears. Studs she had chosen from an impressive collection of gorgeous, sparkling jewels she had tucked away in a velvet box inside her dresser. She turned toward the mirror and smoothed down her perfectly straight blond hair, giving herself an imperious once-over. Ever since I entered the suffocatingly flower-scented room she shared with Rose Sakowitz, she had been directing me, yet she hadn't looked at me once. "And do the sheets nice and tight. I do not want to get into a wrinkly bed."

I drew my hand over her raw silk comforter, evening out the lumps. All I wanted to do was fall into it. This was my fourteenth bed. Rose's would be number fifteen. My own, sixteen. After the vacuuming. Unfortunately, I had a feeling I would never get to my bed as the vacuuming would strike me dead of an aneurysm. Death by Dyson.

"Did you hear me, Glass-licker?" she asked, gracing me with a corner-of-the-eye glance.

"Yes," I told her in my new croaky voice. "Fluff the pillows. No wrinkles."

She turned toward me and took a deep breath. How anyone breathed deeply in the perfumed air of this place was beyond me. "Exactly. I told the girls you'd be good at this," she said, plucking at the cuffs on her pressed Ralph Lauren shirt. "You have that blue-collar air about you."

I stopped short, my hands gripping one of her pillows. I was so stunned, I couldn't even formulate a coherent thought. All I could think was . . . *Kill. Kill. Kill.*

"Cheyenne," Rose scolded, lifting her large leather bag from her desk chair. Rose was a tiny, superskinny girl with chin-length red hair and an orangey tan that was just now starting to fade. I had no idea how that big bag of hers didn't just pull her right down. "Don't listen to her," she told me.

I forced myself to smile at Rose, then melted Cheyenne's fourth layer of Estée Lauder base with my eyes.

"What? I was just paying her a compliment!" Cheyenne said. "You knew that, right, Glass-licker?"

"Sure," I said with a tight smile. "I'd rather have a blue collar than a silver spoon up my ass," I whispered under my breath.

Cheyenne's face clouded over, but she quickly recovered. "Someone has an attitude," she said smoothly. "Whatever shall we do to teach her her place?"

She picked up a big pot of pink blush beads and turned them over on the white-and-green flowered area rug in the center of the hardwood floor. "Oh! Oops!"

"Cheyenne!" Rose cried.

She responded by lifting her heel and grinding the little pellets into the thick weave. Part of me wanted to grab her by her perfect hair and grind her face in there as well. But of course I did not.

"You can clean that up when you're done, Glass-licker," Cheyenne said. "Unless you want me to tell Noelle how clever you are."

She turned and walked out. Rose sighed and hesitated by the door.

"You don't have to worry about that now. There's always tonight," she said. "And don't take too much time on my bed. Just throw the covers over it in case Noelle checks."

"She checks?" I asked.

Rose looked at me pityingly. Clearly I was too naïve for words. "Good luck."

She closed the door quietly behind her, and I listened as her footsteps disappeared down the hall. The dorm was silent as night now. I glanced at the clock. Half an hour to vacuum, shower, get dressed, and get to breakfast. Not that breakfast appealed, but I had to make an appearance or Noelle might put me on toilet duty later. I would have to forgo something to finish in time. Probably the shower.

With a sigh, I moved to Rose's bed. She'd been nice, so I'd do better than just flipping the covers up. I straightened the sheets and comforter and then lifted the pillows. There was something jammed between the corner of the bed and the wall. I placed my knee in the center of the mattress and took a closer look. Whatever it was was kind of crumply and green and—"Oh, my God."

My hand flew over my mouth. It was a piece of a muffin. An old, moldy corn muffin and its wrapper that Rose had obviously stuffed there after snacking on it one night. One night in early September from the looks of it. Apparently even the crème de la crème could be slobs. I turned around, stumbled into their bathroom, and slammed my kneecaps against the linoleum as I doubled over.

Nothing like a nice, long dry heave into the bowl to get the day started just right.

crudge

By the time I arrived at the sun-drenched cafeteria, those girls who dared to risk their perfect figures were ready for seconds and it was my job to fill their orders. Although the last thing I wanted to do was look at food, I found myself piling two trays high with toast, doughnuts, fruit, and drinks.

"Eggs?" the man behind the counter offered, lifting a spoonful of yellow scrambled goo.

I winced. "No, thanks."

I grabbed myself a bagel and added it to the growing pile, hoping I might be able to choke some of it down. Up ahead, a pair of freshman boys was chatting up a pretty freshman girl with dark, curly hair. She giggled and preened and I sneered. Oh, to be that carefree and awake. And clean.

"I heard that last year all the freshman girls who went came back with tattoos," one of the boys said. "The virgins got *V*'s and the nonvirgins got lip prints. Right on their left cheeks," he said, checking out the girl's butt in her pleated mini.

"I thought no one came back from the Legacy a virgin," she said, dipping her spoon into her yogurt then sucking on it teasingly as the line edged forward.

Instantly my ears perked up. The Legacy. Hadn't Dash and those guys mentioned that last night? My memory of the previous evening was hazy, but I did remember them saying something about how Thomas would never miss it. How he'd be there no matter what. How did these kids know about it?

"Not that you have to worry about that, right, Gwen?" the other boy said, practically licking his lips.

"Maybe," she said, lifting her tray and turning toward them. "Maybe not."

She traipsed off, leaving the boys gaping behind her. "Dude, I am so gonna hit that at the Legacy. Just wait," one of them said.

"I will," the other said grumpily.

"Oh! That's right! You won't be there, will you, Mills!?" the first kid taunted. "Poor, poor frosh. Maybe your grandkids will get to go."

With that, the kid laughed and sauntered toward his table, head thrown back all the way.

So the Legacy was an exclusive party. One that Gwen and Boy Toy #1 could go to but Boy Toy #2 could not. I would have to file this information away for later and try to process it when my brain was actually functioning again.

I took a deep breath and smelled the scent of fresh paint behind me an instant before I felt the warmth of a body. I turned around to find a bright-eyed Josh Hollis smiling down at me.

Instantly my shoulder muscles coiled with tension. I couldn't look at Josh without thinking of Thomas and wondering whether or not Josh had heard from him.

"Ouch. You look like crudge," Josh said.

"Crudge?"

"I make up words when no existing terms seem fit to rise to the occasion," Josh said. "Therefore, crudge."

"Well, I'm honored to have inspired a new word," I lied. Not that I could blame him. My dirty-ass hair was back in a slick-from-grease ponytail and I was sure there was a nice, green undertone to my waxy skin.

"Are you okay?" Josh asked as we moved forward in line. "I was a little worried about you last night."

The dim memory of a stone-faced Josh flitted through my mind. One more thing I had forgotten about until now. Come to think of it, though, why would *Josh* be worried about me? We barely knew each other. A hopeful thought occurred to me in a rush.

"Did Thomas ask you to look out for me or something?" I asked.

Josh blinked. "No. Thomas didn't say anything to me before he left, actually."

"Oh. So you really have no idea where he is?" I asked.

"No. You?"

"No."

I moved ahead, my heart pounding woefully.

"Typical Thomas," Josh said under his breath.

"What?" I asked.

"Nothing. It's just . . . you'd think he'd at least let *you* know where he's going," he said with major emphasis on the *you*. So he did know what Thomas and I had done. Or he suspected. Or maybe not. Maybe he just knew I meant a lot to Thomas. At least, I thought I did.

How was it that our relationship was even more confusing without him here than it was when he was around?

"But I should have known," Josh continued. "He's never been one for thinking of other people."

I swallowed hard. This morning had already been too much for me to handle. I didn't need to add "picking apart my missing boyfriend" to the list. "Let's talk about something else," I said.

"Right. Sorry," he told me with an apologetic smile. "I'm sure he'll call you. Eventually."

Feeling warm and conspicuous, I glanced around for a new topic.

"So what's all that?" I asked, gesturing at his tray. It was piled even higher than my own two. "Bulking up for winter?"

"Nah. Some of the guys were still hungry, so . . ." He shrugged.

"I don't get it," I said.

"Get what?" he asked, lifting a chocolate-chip muffin onto the tray.

"Why are you always doing stuff for them?" I said. "It's not like you have to."

Like some people.

"I have four younger brothers and sisters and only one older brother, who was allergic to helping out," he replied, shoving his hand into the back pocket of his baggy, paint-stained jeans as he pushed his tray forward on the slide rail with the other. "I think doing stuff for people is hardwired into my brain."

I picked up a bowl for cereal. "Ah."

"Why do *you* do it?" he asked.

"Uh, they make me," I said automatically.

Josh eyed me dubiously. "Huh?"

I blinked. He didn't know? He didn't know I was an indentured servant of Billings House? I thought this was public knowledge, this systematic hazing. At least the stuff I'd done before I had moved in had been noticed by others. Dash, in particular, had made it clear that he enjoyed my suffering. How could Josh not know?

"Wait. What're they making you do?" he asked.

Red alert. Flashing lights. Yellow caution tape. If he didn't know, maybe he wasn't *supposed* to know.

Fuck.

"Oh, nothing," I said with a shrug, my heartbeat pounding in my temples.

"Reed—"

"*Josh*," I replied.

Suddenly, understanding lit his eyes. "You can't tell me." He smirked, trying to make light. "Or you could tell me, but then you'd have to kill me."

I lifted both trays awkwardly from the slide rails and balanced them on my palms. "Don't worry about it," I told him.

"Well, if it's bad you could always spit in their coffee," he said.

I looked down at the steaming mugs on one of the trays. Damn that would be nice. "Uh, no," I said.

"Well, just . . . be careful," he said. "I mean, don't let them make you do anything, you know—"

Crazy? Dangerous? Stupid? Done, done, and done.

"I won't." I paused as one of the coffee mugs teetered.

"Here. Let me help you," Josh offered, reaching for the heavier of the trays.

"Thanks, but I—"

I glanced up at our table and instantly everything inside of me dropped. Walt Whittaker, big as a mountain on a clear day, sat at the end of the table. Flashes hit me like machine-gun fire to the skull.

My hands on his chest. Warm brown eyes. A handkerchief. Thick arms. Rough lips. Tongue, tongue, tongue. And—ow. A twinge in my chest.

Holy crap. Had I let that person feel me up?

"Hey! Watch it!" Josh said.

He grabbed the tray seconds before it went over. One of the doughnuts slid off the tray and plopped, icing side down, onto the floor.

"I gotta go," I told him. Then I dropped the second tray on the nearest table and was out of there for my second dry heave of the day.

judgment day

I arrived for morning services seconds before the doors closed. All over the chapel, people were engaged in intense, hushed, conversation, and I heard Thomas's name more than once. Dozens of eyes followed my progress up the aisle and the whispering intensified in my wake. Apparently, Thomas's disappearance had become the topic of the moment, and since he wasn't here to gawk at, it seemed I had been nominated for the job. The girlfriend. The one left behind. She who must be watched.

Suddenly I was glad that I'd had to heave and miss breakfast. If I'd stayed in the cafeteria, I might have been mobbed. At least here, no one could approach me. For the moment, I could regroup.

Ducking my head, I slid into a small space at the end of one of the sophomore pews, next to my least favorite person at Easton, Missy Thurber. Having spent the rest of the breakfast period sitting in the infirmary sipping apple juice, I was feeling just slightly more like myself. Then Missy started sniffing elaborately through her tunnel-like nostrils, sampling the air. She leaned toward me, sniffed again, and groaned.

"Ugh! Where did you sleep last night?" she asked, pinching her nose. "In the landscaper's shed?"

I flushed scarlet as she got up, stepped over my former room-mate, Constance Talbot, and forced her to slide over next to me.

"Hey," Constance whispered uncertainly. I hadn't seen much of her since I had deserted her for Billings two days earlier. Her curly red hair was twisted into two long braids. She already looked young for her age with her freckles and roundish face. Now she looked twelve. "How's everything?" she asked.

"Fine."

Except my boyfriend is AWOL, I drunkenly sucked face with a stranger, I have a hangover the size of Yugoslavia, and I'm about to starve to death.

"Everyone's talking about Thomas. Have you heard from him?" she asked. She looked both concerned for me and hopeful that she might be granted an inside scoop.

"No," I said. "How are *you*?" I asked, mostly to change the topic.

"Well, I have a single," she said with a sad smile. Constance was a social being, not the type of person who would thrive in a single, and we both knew it. I wanted to say something to make her feel better about my total desertion, but I could think of nothing. It wasn't like I was coming back. No matter how many chores the Billings Girls made me do, living in the most exclusive dorm on campus was still a huge improvement over living in Bradwell. All the girls who lived in Billings had perfect lives—they were popular, successful, straight-A students who went on to great things. That was going to be me now. If they didn't work me to death first.

"Are you okay?" Constance asked, studying me closely.

"Yeah. Fine. Just a little tired."

At the microphone, Dean Marcus cleared his throat, saving me from further questioning.

"Good morning, students," he said, gripping both sides of the podium with his craggly fingers. "This morning I am going to dispense with the pleasantries, as we have a bit of serious business at hand. No doubt you all know by now that one of our own, Thomas Pearson, has gone missing from campus."

My empty stomach turned and contracted. Murmurs rose to the rafters of the chapel as this most juicy rumor was finally authority-figure confirmed.

"Figures they'd wait till after all the parents are gone to actually bring this little tidbit up," someone said behind me.

"Silence, please!" Dean Marcus called out, raising one hand.

And silence instantly fell.

"This is a not a matter we are taking lightly," he continued. "As no one has come forward with any information as to Mr. Pearson's whereabouts, I have asked the chief of Easton Township police, Chief Sheridan, to speak to you. Please give the chief your undivided attention."

He turned to a gray-haired gentleman in a stiff blue suit who was seated behind him. "Chief Sheridan?"

Pews creaked all over the chapel as everyone strained for a good look at the chief. He towered over Dean Marcus as he approached the microphone, his shoulders as square as his jaw. When he swallowed I could see his large Adam's apple bob, even from rows back.

"Thank you, Dean Marcus," the chief said, his voice grave. He looked out at all of us with steely blue eyes and I could see the displeasure he was feeling as he addressed us. I wondered if he resented the school for being nestled within his jurisdiction, if Thomas's disappearance was a headache with which he'd rather not cope. Or if it was on some level exciting for him. My guess was that not much happened around this sleepy, upscale town. Maybe he was eager to solve an actual case.

"I'm sorry to have to come here under such grave circumstances," the chief began. "Now, this is a big school. I'm sure that some of you know Thomas Pearson, while some of you do not."

I felt a warm hand cover mine. I looked down to find Constance's fingers gripping my own in a comforting way. My first instinct was to slide my hand away, but I didn't. She was trying to be a good friend. I needed all the friendliness I could get these days.

"But this week we will be interviewing *all* of you," the chief said.

Another wave of whispers met this announcement. The vibe in the room was almost excited. What was wrong with these people? Didn't they realize the implications of this? The police thought something bad had happened to Thomas. They thought one of us might have something to do with it. How did that translate into excitement?

"Please, when we come to get you out of class, do not be nervous," the chief continued. "Understand that we are not treating any of you as suspects. All we care about right now is finding your class-mate and returning him to his parents safely."

So they can browbeat him into submission and ship him off to mil-itary school, no doubt.

"There will be no judgments," he added. "But we *will* be grate-ful for any light you can shed on the situation."

His eyes fell on me as he said this and I sank a bit lower in my seat. *Why look at me? Why?*

He's not. He's just looking in this general direction. Get a grip.

"I thank you in advance for your cooperation."

The chief pushed himself away from the podium and leaned down to whisper something to the dean. It was all the pause the student body needed before breaking into full pandemonium.

"Do you think he bailed?"

"Maybe he was kidnapped."

"I bet that freak Marco knows where he is. You think the police have talked to him yet?"

"Why would they? No one in the administration knows where he got his shit. They're so oblivious."

Marco? Who the hell is Marco?

I squirmed, trying to ignore all the voices around me. I tried even harder to ignore the implications of what they were saying—that it seemed that these random girls might actually know more about Thomas than I did.

"Please. I bet the kid just scored some tainted shit and is lying in a pool of his own vomit somewhere."

Okay. That was it. Suddenly, all the morbid thoughts I had been trying to keep at bay for the past two days hit my already fragile skull with the force of a freight train. In that moment, the feeble hope that Thomas was fine was all but obliterated. My heart pounded shallowly and, panicked, I leaned forward to press my forehead into the cool back rail of the pew in front of mine. The sour taste in my mouth intensified.

Breathe. Just breathe.

I could sense everyone looking at me. Could feel their curious, intrigued stares.

"Reed. Are you okay? Do you want me to take you to the infirmary?" Constance asked, laying her hand on my back.

"Take her to a shower first," Missy suggested helpfully.

Breathe. Breathe. Breathe.

Kidnapped. Tainted. Vomit.

Where the hell was Thomas? Where the *hell* had he gone?

the girlfriend

The whispers followed me out of the pew and all the way back down the aisle after services. I crossed my arms over my stomach and held on tight, trying to keep all the nervousness and fear and total conspicuousness I felt from bursting out of me in all directions. Thomas was missing. Thomas was missing and the police were looking at all of us like we were suspects. And as if that wasn't bad enough, now the entire school was watching me too.

Why couldn't he just come back? If Thomas could just show his face for five seconds on campus, all of this would go away. I just wanted it to go away.

Ariana and Taylor stepped away from the arched doorway to the chapel as I approached and I was relieved to see friendly faces, even if they were the same faces that had dragged me out of bed and into an apron that morning. My grip on my own elbows even loosened a bit.

But then Taylor whispered something quickly to Ariana, cast me an almost skittish look, ducked her head, and speed-walked off across the quad. I wondered if she was feeling guilty about what she and her friends had done to me earlier. She had, after all, always displayed a tad more of a conscience than the rest of the Billings Girls.

"But I heard they broke up. . . ."

"I know, but they got back together, like, the *day* he disappeared. . . . "

I glared over my shoulder and two sophomore girls I recognized from class quickly blushed scarlet and hurried away. Ariana fell into step next to me and I was glad to have her there. My gossip buffer.

"Everything all right?" she asked.

"Sure," I said, feigning nonchalance. Something told me Ariana would appreciate the show of strength. "What's with Taylor?"

"Oh, she's still not feeling well," Ariana replied.

"Hangover?" I whispered.

"Among other things." Ariana sighed. "Taylor gets strep every fall and then is sick on and off all the way through the winter until spring finally springs again. She spends half her time studying in the infirmary. Better get used to it." She stared off after Taylor's retreating form. "Weak constitution on that girl," she said almost wistfully. "It's a shame."

"Oh." I stared at the ground. Being sick and infirmary-bound seemed like a fine option to me just then. *Maybe I should get Taylor to breathe on me*, I thought.

"You okay?" Ariana asked me.

"I guess," I replied.

Even though I wasn't. Even though my body, heart, and soul all ached with a vengeance. Even though I felt as if I could break apart from frustration and confusion. Why couldn't Thomas just call me? Or Josh? Or anyone? *Why was he doing this to us?*

Was it because the whispers were right? Had something horrible actually happened to him? A chill raced down my back and I squirmed, moving my shoulders around, trying to shake it. Ariana watched every move I made as if each one held the key to my soul.

"So. What are you going to tell them?" Ariana asked, her piercing blue eyes full of pointed concern.

"Who?"

"The police," Ariana said in a low voice.

I paused. "What do you mean?"

Ariana turned and stepped so close to me I could have counted the pores on her nose if she'd had any. Her skin was as perfect as porcelain.

Porcelain. Toilets. Bile. Ugh.

"I mean, you're Thomas's girlfriend. They're definitely going to ask you a lot of questions," Ariana said. "You'd better know what you're going to say before you go in there."

My throat went dry. For a moment I felt like I was completely outside my body. She could not mean what I thought she meant. A cool breeze lifted her white-blond hair and caused her scarf to dance. Behind her some guy shouted at another. Ariana didn't move or flinch or blink.

"Ariana . . . I don't know where Thomas is," I said finally.

Ariana stared into my eyes, searching. Searching so thoroughly that heat started to prickle all over my body. So thoroughly that I found myself wondering if I *did* have something to hide.

The moment I thought that, Ariana smiled.

"Okay," she said finally.

"What?"

"Nothing. But if you do want to talk before you go in there, just let me know."

"Thanks," I said.

Slowly, Ariana backed away. "I'd better get to class."

She lifted one shoulder and gave me a small, knowing glance before turning and strolling off. Left alone again, I couldn't help but notice all the stares. Whenever my eyes fell on someone else, they quickly looked away. Whenever I got near anyone, they instantly stopped talking. Was this what it was going to be like for me now? Everyone talking about me all the time and watching my every move? I had known from the moment I arrived at Easton that I didn't just want to disappear among the nobodies, but I had never wanted this.

I checked my watch as I headed across the quad. Ten minutes left before class. I needed a friendly ear. Someone who could calm me down and remind me why I was here. I dropped onto the nearest bench, pulled out my cell, and dialed my brother, who was miles upon miles away at Penn State. He picked up on the fifth ring.

"Hello?"

"Scott? It's Reed. Did I wake you up?"

"No! No! I don't have a class for another three hours, but hey, I'm wide awake," he said.

I smirked. A group of girls was watching me from a few feet away so I stared back at them until they were shamed into looking away.

"How's everything there?" I asked.

"Fine. How's everything at Eat Me Academy?" he asked.

"Ha ha. So glad I got all the intelligence in the family."

"At least I got the stunning good looks," he said. "So what's wrong?"

"Something has to be wrong?"

"In this family, yes," he said.

I blew out a sigh. "It's gotten really weird around here," I told him. "This . . . well, this guy has gone missing and the cops are all over the place now. They're gonna interview everyone."

"Missing? Like kidnapped or something?" Scott asked.

"I don't know," I said, swallowing hard.

"Do you know this guy?" he asked.

"Kind of." *Like in the biblical sense.* "He's a friend."

"Wow. That sucks. But I'm sure he'll show up," he said. "I bet people disappear from that place all the time, then turn up on exotic cruise ships or something."

I laughed.

"What? Isn't that what rich people do? I remember Felicia saying something about some dude inviting the entire senior class to his palatial estate in Turks and Caicos or something."

Felicia. Right. My older brother's older and cooler girlfriend.

How had I forgotten that Scott knew someone who had gone here? She was the whole reason I had looked into Easton in the first place. She had spent her junior and senior years here at Easton before graduating and heading off to Dartmouth. Which meant, of course, that she knew everything about this place.

"Hey, speaking of Felicia," I said, settling in, "did she ever mention anything to you about the Legacy?"

"The Legacy? No. Doesn't sound familiar. What is it?"

"Some party, I think. I don't know. Everyone's talking about it, though."

"So why don't you ask someone about it?" Scott asked.

"I don't want to look like a loser," I told him. It was a relief to actually say it. A relief to talk to someone I could be honest with.

"Too late," he joked.

"You're funny," I told him flatly.

"Whatever. Look, I better go. I'm annoying Todd," he said. I imagined my brother's roommate groaning and pulling a pillow over his head. "But listen, you should call Dad later."

Instantly, guilt twisted at my heart. I hadn't called my father in days.

"Why? So he can make me feel guilty without even trying?"

"I got news for you. I've been taking psych. Apparently we get to feel guilty for the rest of our lives. Might as well get used to it."

I sighed. "Fine. I'll call him."

"He misses you. So does Mom, in her own sick and twisted way," Scott said.

Suddenly all I wanted to do was get off the phone. But he'd

done his job. He'd reminded me full force of why I was here—of who I was running away from.

"Whatever. Go back to sleep," I told him, getting up. "I'll talk to you later."

"Later," he said.

And the line went dead.

I sighed and turned my steps toward class, ignoring the murmurs that followed my path. Better get used to those, too. Better get used to a lot of things.

mean girls

"So, what are you wearing to the Legacy this year?"

I paused on my way out of the campus bookstore, clutching the box of pens I had just purchased. It seemed that when the entire campus wasn't talking about me it was talking about the Legacy. Maybe it wouldn't be too hard to find out about it on my own.

"I don't know. I was thinking the black Chanel."

Sitting on a bench just a few feet away were two girls I recognized from Bradwell—two glossy-haired, skinny chicks whose cell phones were permanently attached to their ears. Even as they spoke, one of them held her phone to her ear, the mouthpiece away from her mouth, while the other one texted on her own sleek number. I dropped to the ground and pretended to tie my shoe.

"Didn't you wear that to, like, your mother's wedding last year?" the blonder girl asked the less blond girl.

"Yeah. So?"

"So? You were photographed!" Blonder said. "You cannot wear a dress in which you were already photographed to the Legacy. It is just not done."

Less Blond nodded thoughtfully. "You're right. What was I thinking?"

Then Blonder's slate eyes fell on me. "Uh, excuse me? Do we amuse?"

"Sorry," I replied, standing. "What exactly is the Legacy?"

The two girls exchanged an incredulous look. "No place we'll ever see you," Less Blond said, dialing her phone. "Even if you *are* in Billings."

"Dana! You're so bad!" Blonder said, shoving Less Blond's arm.

My face turned pink. "What the hell does that mean?"

"It means," Less Blond said, "don't act like just because Billings took you in you're somehow better than the rest of us. We all know where you came from, scholarship girl."

"Don't worry, *somebody* might take pity on you and bring you to the Legacy. You know, since your boyfriend's all MIA."

I swallowed back the huge lump that had formed in my throat. Would it be wrong to actually beat these girls down? I'd never actually gotten into a fist fight before, but with all the psychotic emotions roiling around inside my chest, they had picked the wrong time to mess with me. The thought of jumping Less Blond actually crossed my incoherent mind. I could even hear the exact pitch of her surprised screech, see her cell phone flying into the air and cracking on the stone path. It was not an unamusing visual.

I stood up straight, not entirely sure what I was going to do. They both looked up at me. I could tell Blonder was about to say something even snarkier, but then both of them blanched. Had I just sprung horns or something?

"I have to go," Blonder said.

It wasn't until they had both gotten up and scurried off that I felt a presence behind me. Somehow I wasn't surprised when I turned around and saw Noelle just coming to a stop.

"Oh. Did I scare off your little friends?" she asked, arching an eyebrow.

"Apparently," I said. "Thanks for that."

"Anytime," she told me. "Girls have to learn their place."

"What do you mean?" I asked, my heart still pounding.

"I mean *they* don't get to mess with you, Glass-licker," she said, slinging her arm over my shoulder. "That's *my* job."

I actually managed a laugh.

"So. How are you holding up?" Noelle asked. "You must be so sick of all this Pearson crap already."

My heart turned over, as it did at every mention of Thomas. "Aren't you worried about him at all?" I asked.

Noelle slipped away from me and looked me in the eye. As always, she was nearly impossible to read. "Reed, Thomas Pearson has a way of always landing on his feet."

"If you say so," I replied.

"You cannot listen to what all the little idiots with no lives around here are saying," she said adamantly. "Look at Dash and Gage. They've known Pearson their entire lives and they're not worried. Why? Because they *know* him. And they know that he's out there somewhere having a big fat laugh at our expense."

I smirked sadly at the thought. "You think?"

"I *know*," Noelle replied, hooking her arm through mine. "Stop worrying about him. Because sooner or later he's going to show up here like it's one big joke and then you are going to be *so* pissed you wasted your time."

I took a deep breath and let her words sink in. Thomas was fine. All his friends—the people who knew him best—believed he was fine. They even believed he was going to show up at that Legacy thing all ready to party. Who was I to doubt their certainty?

"So. Ready for a little kick-ass soccer practice?" Noelle asked. "I promise I won't lay you out today. Wait. Actually, I don't."

I laughed as we headed off toward Billings to change. A little kick-ass soccer practice was exactly what I needed.

"What were you crazy kids talking about anyway?" Noelle asked. "Looked serious."

For a split second I considered asking her about the Legacy. But I wasn't yet desperate enough to remind Noelle that I knew so little about the inner workings of this place. I'd just have to keep trying to find out on my own.

"Oh, you know, the latest in Vera Wang," I said blithely as we turned up the path to Billings.

Noelle laughed for a long time. "That's what I like about you, Reed," she said between gasps for air. "Sometimes you really slay me."

dear reed

"Ugh! I just cannot take this sweater one more second," London Simmons said, pulling a creamy white cashmere sweater over her head and tossing it at her silver garbage can. Her dark brown hair grazed her bare back, falling into perfect waves.

"London! You cannot just throw away cashmere," her roommate, Vienna Clark, replied.

London and Vienna, or "the Twin Cities," as the rest of Billings called them, were two very buxom, very big-haired socialites who had apparently been friends forever. They had summoned me to their room the moment I had gotten back from dinner because they needed some help "feng shui—ing," as London had put it, which actually meant they wanted me to organize their shoes by color, then by heel height. At the moment, I was on the floor, doing exactly that.

"At least donate it or something," Vienna suggested.

London, who was admiring her double-D's in the mirror, turned to look at me.

"Sorry," she said, plucking the sweater out of the can. "Did you want this?"

Her brown eyes were completely innocent. She blinked, waiting for my excited reply.

"Uh, no thanks," I said flatly.

"Not to her! To the *needy*!" Vienna said, rolling her eyes as she picked up her nail file and walked over. "Don't mind her, Glass-licker," she told me, pulling the sweater out of London's fingers. "The skinnier she gets, the dumber she gets."

I smirked.

"Omigosh! You're just jealous!" London said, swiping at Vienna.

They both settled back on their beds again to continue their primping rituals. I yanked another pair of red shoes out of the back of the closet and lined them up with all the other red shoes, comparing heel heights. I was almost done. Then I could finally, *finally* get back to my room and shower.

"I saw Walt Whittaker on campus today," London said casually.

Instantly, all the hair on the back of my neck stood on end. Somehow I had managed to avoid Whit all day. Every time he saw me he blushed and looked away. Apparently he was just as embarrassed by our encounter as I was. He'd spent most of our mealtimes chatting with professors over at their tables, something I'd never seen a single student do before, and outside the caf I hadn't seen him at all. But did the Twin Cities know that we had hooked up?

"V, I am so going to make him mine."

Apparently not.

Vienna snorted a laugh. "Please. Every other girl on this campus is gonna be after Whittaker in the next couple of weeks."

Wha-huh? *Why*?

"So? You don't think I can get him?" London asked incredulously.

"You've got as good a shot as anyone else," Vienna replied.
"But no one knows what goes on inside that thick head.
Personally, I've always thought he was gay."

I stifled a laugh and shoved the last pair of red shoes into place.
If he was gay it would certainly account for his lack of skills in the
feeling-up department.

"Just because he's gay doesn't mean I can't use him," London
said.

Then they both laughed. I pushed myself up and slapped my
hands on my apron. Part of me was dying to know what London
wanted to use Whit for. Money? Doubtful. Everyone around here
had more than they knew what to do with. But an even bigger part
of me was dying to get the hell out of there. Plus I had a feeling they
wouldn't tell me anyway.

"All done," I said.

"You're excused," London said dismissively.

I shot her a look of death that she didn't even notice, then
turned and walked out. I practically ran down the dimly lit hall to
my room, blowing by all the black-and-white framed photos of
Billings "Through the Ages." At some point I had appreciated the
beautiful touches of Billings, the gleaming woodwork, the thick

carpeting, the bronze wall sconces, the French windows at either end of each hallway. But now all I saw was more stuff to clean, more to scrub, more to wax. I couldn't get back to my room and away from it all fast enough. My hand was on the doorknob when I heard someone enter the hall behind me.

"Miss Brennan."

I stopped and closed my eyes. So close.

Mrs. Lattimer, the middle-aged house mother of Billings House, approached me at a broken pace, her stride hindered by her skinny pencil skirt. Her dark hair was pulled back in a bun and her white shirt was, as always, buttoned all the way up, with three strands of pearls sitting on top. Mrs. Lattimer was skinny and pointy; her skin was rough as leather. She was never seen without a thick layer of eyeliner and mascara, as if she thought drawing attention to her watery eyes would cause the average person to miss the rather large birthmark on her chin. I had met her on my first night at Billings and she had looked me over as if confused by my very existence. I had avoided her ever since.

"Miss Brennan, I understand that you made all the beds this morning," she said, her craggly hands clasped in front of her.

Wait a minute. She knew about that?

"You somehow, however, overlooked my own," she said, lifting her chin. "I would appreciate it if you afforded me the same courtesy you have the other women of this dorm."

She was kidding. She had to be kidding. Not only did she know about this hazing ritual, but she *condoned* it? She wanted *in* on it?

"Do I make myself clear?" she asked.

"Uh . . . sure," I said.

"Good," she said with a nod. We both stood there for a long moment. "Well. Go about your business," she said, shooing me with her hand.

"Right. Okay."

I shoved the door open, closed it behind me, and leaned back against it, wishing there was a lock. A bolt. Some kind of alarm system that could alert me to approaching heiresses. I couldn't believe our house mother was in on this. As if I didn't have enough to do already, enough to worry about.

Taking a deep breath, I sank down a bit, unable to move another muscle. My nerves were fried. All day I had been waiting for my classroom doors to open, waiting to be called to Hell Hall to talk to the police. I was completely unable to concentrate and had managed to shred no fewer than ten sheets of loose-leaf into tiny squares. But nothing had happened. The day had ended without a single interruption and now a rumor was floating around that the police were starting with the senior class and working their way down, that they might not even get to us lowly sophomores until late in the week.

Personally, I wanted to get it over with. I felt like my blood had been replaced with pure caffeine. Why didn't they at least come get *me*? Hadn't the crack investigators found out yet that Thomas had a girlfriend?

I pushed away from the door and dropped down on my bed,

looking blankly around my new room. *My new room.* In all the insanity I'd had yet to have the time to fully appreciate the space. It was at least three times bigger than my old room in Bradwell, with a huge arched window overlooking the quad. My desk was immense, with a built-in bulletin board and study lamp, and the double dresser near the wall actually dwarfed the smallish bed. It was also only half full and completely devoid of pictures, jewelry boxes, and knickknacks, unlike every other dresser in this place—which, by the way, were that much more difficult to dust and polish.

Yes, my side of the room was pathetically bare compared to Natasha's, which was replete with posters hung at exact right angles, perfectly organized books and papers, a clear plastic tackle-style box keeping each piece of her incredibly expensive jewelry separate from all the others. But it was home. My home in Billings. I had to remember that. I was here. And all the chores they could throw at me were worth it.

I think.

Finally I shoved myself away from the wall and trudged over to my desk. Some of my books were still in a crate on the floor from when the Billings Girls had gathered them and brought them over. Might as well unpack now while I still had a sliver of energy left in me. I picked up a few of my extra history tomes, which had been assigned to me the first day of school, and lifted them onto the shelf above the desk. The middle one slipped out and fell with a thud to the floor, and try as I might to grab the others, they all slipped and slid and followed, one landing right on my toes.

"Dammit," I said under my breath, dropping to my knees.

I leaned my back into the side of my bed and sighed as several bones cracked and a few muscles uncoiled. Wow, was it nice to be sitting. Maybe the unpacking could wait.

Using a minimal amount of effort, I slid a couple of the books toward me and stacked them in my lap. In doing so, I uncovered a small piece of white paper, folded up tightly, sitting on the hardwood floor. Huh. Where had that come from?

I picked it up and turned it over in my hand. Unfamiliar. Had it fallen out of one of my books? They had all been taken out of the library the first week of school. Maybe it was an old love letter someone had left in there. Intrigued, I unfolded the page. My eye went directly to the signature. The note was computer printed but signed in ink.

By Thomas.

"What?" I said out loud.

Instantly my pulse started to pound in my ears. In my fingertips. In my *eyes.* I pulled my knees up to my chest, scattering the books to the floor, and read, the page trembling in my hands.

Dear Reed,

I'm leaving tonight. I don't know what else to do. A friend of mine knows of this holistic treatment thing where they don't require parental permission. I'm not going to tell you where it is, because I don't want you or anyone else trying to find me. I want to get better. And I don't think I can do that if I stay in touch with the people in my life.

Please don't be mad. It's better for you this way. You're too

good for me. I'm shit for you. You know I am. I love you. I do. But
you deserve better than me. So much better.

I just need some time. Some time on my own, away from my
parents and all the insanity. You understand. I know you do.
You know me better than anyone.

I love you so much, Reed. And I'll miss you. More than you'll
ever know.

Love,
Thomas

Relief flooded through me so quickly and with such force that
my eyes blurred with tears. I wiped them away, and read the note
again. And again. Thomas was all right. He was fine! He wasn't
lying in a pool of his own vomit somewhere; he had gone to get
help. He was out there trying to get well. He was, in fact, better
than he'd ever been.

I took a deep, shaky breath and read the note one more time.
Suddenly a new emotion poisoned the relief, causing the muscles
in my neck to tense. Thomas had broken up with me. In a note.
After I'd promised to help him in any way I could, he'd taken off
without so much as a good-bye and hidden a breakup note in my
stuff. What kind of person did that?

Even worse, how could he leave a note in some book and just
trust I would find it? I might have returned this thing to the
library and never seen the note that was tucked away inside. I
might have just gone on worrying forever. He could have just

called. Just a five-second call and he could have told me the same thing. Did he not realize the torture he'd put me through?

"Asshole," I groaned, mashing the paper into a ball and throwing it across the room. Who the hell did he think he was, just deciding we were over? Not letting me have a say in anything. Disappearing and making all of us worry. The boy needed help. Serious, professional help.

At least he was getting it.

Two seconds after tossing the note away, I got up and grabbed it from the floor. It wasn't as if I could leave it around for Natasha to find. I flattened it out on my desk and read it one more time.

That was when a new, even more torturous thought occurred to me.

The police. Should I tell the police about this note? Show it to them? Clearly Thomas didn't want me to. He said right there that he was leaving to get away from the insanity—from his parents— and if I told, they would track him down and he would never get the time he needed to get better. But not showing the cops would be like lying. It would be withholding evidence. I could get in serious, serious trouble.

God, I just wished I could talk to him. See him. Hold him. Talk some sense into him. Maybe if I could talk to him I could get him to take responsibility for what he had done. Didn't he realize how much trouble he had caused? Was he that scared of his parents that he thought this was the only way?

I imagined Thomas out there somewhere, alone, trying to deal with his issues, trying to make himself well, and my heart swelled so fast I thought it might pop. I was angry at him, yes, but I also missed him. I also worried about him. I just wished that I could see him and tell him that everything was going to be okay.

And then, yeah, maybe smack him upside the head for doing this to me.

It really is amazing, how closely hate and love are aligned.

"Screw this," I said. I couldn't think about it now. I was too tired. Too emotional. Too inclined to violence. I folded the note, stuffed it in the very back of my desk drawer, and slammed it closed.

Okay. Deep breath. At least I knew Thomas was all right now. At least I knew he was out there somewhere. And if he had any sort of conscience, he'd have to call me eventually. This note was not enough. We needed to talk. Big time.

moral center

After a long shower, and an equally long think, I felt monumentally better. Thomas's note, while it had opened up a huge can of worms, had actually absolved me from a couple of things I had been stressing over. First, he had broken up with me days ago, which technically meant that what I had done in the woods with Whittaker wasn't cheating, which made me feel much better. Second, he was gone from school indefinitely, which meant that I wouldn't have to worry about keeping him and the Billings Girls in separate corners. I wouldn't have to worry about that anyway, since he had broken up with me.

Yes. I could be very practical about this. Level-headed Reed. That was going to be my new, internal nickname.

That was part one of the plan. Part two of the plan was finding out more about this Legacy thing and getting my ass there so that I could track down Thomas, yell at him for about an hour, and then give him a chance to explain. A very brief chance. After all, Dash had said Thomas would be there no matter what. That Thomas *was* the Legacy. If that was the case, I was sure he wasn't going to let a little holistic treatment get in his way.

I mean, okay, Thomas wasn't good for me. He was probably right about that. Technically, after the first week or so of total bliss, all he'd caused me was confusion, pain, and embarrassment. But that bliss part? That had been *really* good. So good that I had slept with him. And I couldn't just forget about that. He couldn't just take my virginity and slink off into the night leaving nothing but a note. What we had done meant a lot to me, and Thomas needed to know that. He needed to know that I wasn't just going to forget him. That I would *never* forget him, even if we weren't ever going to be together again. I cared about him. And that was that.

I slipped into my terry-cloth robe and cinched it, then grabbed a towel and started rubbing at my hair hard, as if I could rub out all the confusion as well. My head was tipped forward as I walked out of the steamy bathroom, so I didn't see Natasha standing there until I had walked right into her.

"Oh! God! Sorry," I said, jumping back. My free hand flew to my chest and I laughed. "You scared the crap outta me."

Natasha didn't crack a smile. She didn't move. Her stare had "doom" written all over it.

"What?" I said nervously. Had she found the note? Oh, God, had she somehow found the note?

"We need to talk," she said gravely.

"Okay," I said, trying to egg her into a smile with my own. No such luck.

She walked over to her laptop and flipped it open. "Sit," she said, pulling out her desk chair for me.

I shot her a quizzical look but did as I was told. "What're we doing?"

"Just a little slide show," Natasha told me.

She leaned over me, her breast grazing my shoulder and making me flush with embarrassment, and clicked open a window on her computer. What I saw on the screen at first made no sense to me. It was a photograph of what looked like a tongue. A very up-close shot of a tongue being stuck out at the camera. Then suddenly the view went wide and my heart dropped.

It *was* a tongue. My tongue. It was me. And my eyes were half-closed. And I was laughing.

"When did you take this?" I asked, glancing over my shoulder.

"Just watch," she said.

So I did. The next picture featured me chugging a beer in the woods. The next, me with my hands on Whittaker's chest. Me and Whittaker walking away from the clearing together. Me with my arms around Whittaker, my mouth hanging open sloppily, a flask of liquor in my hand. Whittaker with his mouth pressed to mine as I held his face with my hands. Then Whittaker's hand on my breast.

Dread and shame overwhelmed me as I stared at my own face. My head was tipped back and it looked like I was moaning in pleasure, when in fact I had been about to throw up. It made me look like a slut, like a drunken whore who had lured some guy out to the woods.

"Why . . . why are you showing these to me?" I asked, as the slideshow started up all over again. I turned my face away, from her, from the screen, from the truth of what I'd done.

"Because I want you to understand how very serious I am about what I am about to propose," Natasha said. She grabbed the chair and spun it around on its wheels so that I had to face her. Bracing her hands on its arms, she leaned forward and looked me dead in the eye. "You do know what these pictures mean, right? You do realize that if I choose to do so, I can get you booted out of here so fast your head will spin."

Tears prickled at the corners of my eyes. She was right, of course. She had photographic evidence of me breaking some very serious school rules. Even worse, it looked as if Whittaker and I had done it all alone. Even though there had been close to a dozen other people in the woods that night, not a single one of them appeared in these pictures.

"Why are you doing this?"

What was wrong with me? I had believed her when she told me she wanted to be my friend. When had I become so gullible?

"Because there's something I need you to do for me," she said, standing up straight.

"What?" I was already her indentured servant. Did we need twisted espionage in our relationship?

"Noelle Lange and her friends are responsible for getting Leanne kicked out of school," Natasha said. "They set her up."

Her accusation did not surprise me. On the day that Natasha's roommate, Leanne Shore, had been escorted from school grounds after being found guilty of breaking the Easton honor code by cheating, Natasha had accused Noelle of having had something to do with it. I had been there, in the quad, when she had gotten right up in Noelle's face. But I had thought Natasha was basically insane.

"How . . . how do you know?" I asked.

"I just know," Natasha said. "The problem is, I have no proof. That's where you come in."

Oh, God, no. No, no, no. Please tell me she isn't going to make me—

"Now that you're our new scrub girl, you have unlimited access to their rooms," Natasha said. "I want you to find the evidence I need. I want you to go through everything they own. They have to have kept something. They're big on trophies. Find me what I need to nail their asses to the wall."

I stared up at her, my hair dripping cold as ice down my neck. "I . . . I can't do that," I said.

I would lose everything. They would find out and they would kick me out of Billings. They would never speak to me again. Everything I had worked for would be gone in an instant.

Plus Noelle would kill me. There was always that.

"Oh, but you can," she said with a smirk. "Unless you want *that* e-mailed to the dean and the board and every single student and teacher at this school."

I glanced up at the screen again. Whittaker's tongue was down my throat. I tasted bile. I tried to swallow but couldn't. Tears stung my eyes all over again. These pictures represented the end of me. The end of my life, my future. Didn't she see that?

"I thought we were friends," I said blankly. Maybe guilt would work. I was grasping at straws.

"Aw! That's so sweet!" Natasha trilled. "So, do we have an understanding?"

I stared at her, hard. There wasn't a trace of regret or uncertainty in her eyes. This was so wrong. Natasha was supposed to be the moral center of Easton. At least, that was what Noelle had once called her, and Natasha had seemed proud of the moniker. Now here she was taking secret soft-core porn shots of her supposed friends and blackmailing people with them. Where was the morality in that?

Of course, she was also president of the Young Republicans club. From everything I'd read and heard my entire life, this was a maneuver of which any politician would be proud.

"Reed? I asked you a question."

My hands were trembling. I couldn't do this. Not after everything Noelle had done for me. Not with everything she could take away.

But Natasha could take away more. And I was looking at the proof of that.

The situation was a perfect lose-lose.

"Yeah. We have an understanding," I said.

"Good. Now get to bed," Natasha told me, mercifully shutting down the slide show. "You've got a lot of work ahead of you."

this

The next morning I methodically moved through my chores, my mind on ten million other things. For some reason, everyone was up and out of their rooms early, and I was able to make the beds without having to endure snide comments or detailed direction. The entire time I was in Noelle and Ariana's room, Natasha's voice played like a skipping CD in my mind.

Nail their asses to the wall . . . nail their asses to the wall . . . nail their asses to the wall . . .

I stared at Noelle's dresser. It taunted me, begging me to rifle through its drawers. No one was around. It would only take a few minutes. If Natasha made good on her threats, it would mean a one-way ticket back to Croton, Pennsylvania, and my prescription-drug-addict mother and my depressed father. It would mean the end of everything.

And yeah, if I found the proof she was looking for, not only would Noelle and the others hate me, but they would also get thrown out of school. They would be gone and I would still be here, in Billings. Even without them, I would still have a chance, right?

They might have been the most powerful of the Billings Girls, but I would still have the Billings name behind me. That had to count for something. Didn't it?

So, really, what did I have to lose?

I started for the dresser, but the moment I did, a sickening dread came over me. I couldn't do it. I couldn't look through their private things. I couldn't help Natasha rat out Noelle and Ariana— the only people who had shown any real concern for me since Thomas left. Yeah, they made me do chores, but they were also my friends. Sort of. And besides, it was just wrong. So I told myself I didn't have time—that I would deal with it later—and I moved on.

After my shower I pulled my damp hair back into a ponytail, grabbed my books, and rushed out. That was when I heard the party.

"Omigod! *Look* at this luggage! This is divine!"

"Open the big one! The big one!"

A champagne bottle popped and a bunch of girls squealed. What was going on downstairs? It sounded like a bad episode of *The Bachelor*. I slowly walked down the carpeted steps and paused. The entire entry room was filled with white helium balloons. All the girls of Billings were gathered around a pile of elaborately decorated gifts in the center of the floor, while already-opened boxes had been flung against the walls. Wrapping paper littered the room and ribbons had been strung from the banister and the wall hangings. I saw Kiran slip a silk scarf around her neck and tip a glass of champagne down her throat.

It was seven thirty in the morning.

"What's going on?" I asked, arriving at the bottom stair.

"Glass-licker! Just the girl I was looking for!" Kiran trilled. She grabbed a small box and handed it to me with a flourish. "For you!"

It was an iPod. A limited-edition sequined aqua iPod.

"What? Why?"

Everyone laughed.

"It's Kiran's birthday!" Taylor announced, looking more rosy-cheeked than she had in days. Everyone whooped and hollered.

"It is? Happy birthday!" I told her with a smile.

"And on Kiran's birthday, we *all* get gifts," Vienna told me, sipping her champagne.

"I don't get it," I said.

"Every year it's the same thing," Kiran said, rolling her eyes. "All these presents roll in from designers and photographers and magazine editors and stylists. So much crap I can't even fit it all in my room."

"And there are always *tons* of duplicates," Noelle said, fingering a Louis Vuitton purse.

"So I give it all away," Kiran said, throwing her hands up with a smile. "Or most of it, anyway. I think I'm keeping the luggage."

"Oh," Rose said, pouting. She had clearly been coveting the five-bag set, hovering over it ever since I arrived.

"So that's for you," Kiran said, gesturing at me with her champagne glass.

"Really? Even Cinderella gets a gift?" I joked.

Kiran and Noelle looked at each other and laughed. "Even Cinderella," Noelle said.

Ah. So that was it. No one else wanted it, so I got it. Still, I couldn't complain. I was impressed that they had thought of me at all.

"Get over here!" Kiran said, throwing her arm around me and pulling me toward the gift pile. "There has to be some more good stuff that hasn't been claimed. Everyone clear out! Let Glass-licker pick something!"

There were a few grumbles, but the girls backed off. I eyed the pile of designer tags, little blue boxes with white bows, big black boxes with gold ribbon. These were Kiran's gifts. Kiran's things. And she was offering to share it all. With me. No strings attached.

"Here! This color would look *amazing* on you, Reed," Taylor said, holding up a silky red dress.

"Take the suede jacket. Every girl needs a little suede," Ariana said, handing over a box.

"We'll make a fashionista out of you yet," Kiran told me, offering a champagne flute.

"Wow. This is incredible, Kiran. Thanks," I said.

"Well," she said, stepping in front of me and looking me in the eye. "What are friends for?"

My insides squeezed with guilt and I took a slug of the champagne. Friends, huh? What would she think if she knew that a few minutes ago I had been considering pawing through her stuff? And Noelle's and Ariana's and Taylor's? Would she still call me a friend then? Not likely.

I shook my head and tried to clear the negativity. I hadn't done it. I hadn't betrayed them. Not yet anyway. But for the first time, as I looked around at their eager, happy faces, I suddenly realized what I had to lose if I went through with Natasha's plan. It was this. If I went through with it, these girls would all be gone from this place, gone from my life.

I had this to lose.

perfect gentleman

All throughout my morning classes, I was in a daze. If my art teacher had called on me during her lecture about French Impressionism, I probably would have muttered an answer like, "The ratio of the height to the hypotenuse." I had no idea where I was.

To spy or not to spy? That was the question. And when that wasn't the question, there was always that other infinitesimal issue: When were the police going to come get me? And when they did, was I or was I not going to tell them about Thomas's note?

I had a few more pressing things on my mind than whether or not Claude Monet could be considered a revolutionary.

When I was finally released from my fourth class of the day, I was the first one out the door. I practically jogged down the hallway, in desperate need of oxygen. I had to clear my head. I had to go somewhere and think. I had no idea what any of my teachers had said all morning long. If I didn't figure all this out soon, Natasha's blackmail would be a moot point. I would flunk out before she could get me expelled.

As I shoved open the door of the classroom building and emerged into the sun, I took a nice deep breath of the crisp autumn air. This was what I needed. I would stroll at a leisurely pace across campus to the cafeteria. I would take a second to breathe and regroup. A few minutes of alone time were just what the shrink ordered.

"Hello, Reed."

Walt Whittaker was leaning up against the stone pillar at the bottom of the stairs. Instantly Natasha's nasty slide show replayed itself in my brain. Lips, hands, tongues. Ugh. Apparently he had finally decided it was time to talk to me. The boy officially had my nomination for the Worst Timing Award.

"Hi," I said, walking right by him.

As always, a few gossiping girls were watching me and I was hoping he would be embarrassed in front of them and take the hint. I physically shuddered as I passed him. What should have been a quickly forgotten, detail-fuzzy hookup had now turned into a messy encounter that was permanently burned into my brain.

"I was hoping we could talk."

With his long legs, he had caught up to me in two simple strides.

I took a deep breath and let it out audibly. Okay. This was not his fault. He wasn't the one blackmailing me. As far as I knew he didn't even have a clue that those pictures existed. And it wasn't as if I could avoid the guy forever. *Might as well get this over with*, I thought. At least it would be one less thing to think about. I stepped off the cobbled path and under the shade of a golden maple.

I tried not to cringe when I looked at him.

"How are you?" Whittaker asked me, his brown eyes full of concern.

"Fine," I told him. "You?"

"I'm well. Thank you for asking. Listen, about the other night," he began, causing my insides to squirm. "I wanted to apologize. I was a tad over my limit and I think you may have been as well." He looked at me for confirmation.

"A tad."

Understatement of the millennium.

"Well, I think I may have taken advantage," he said, looking down briefly at his loafers. "And for that I am truly sorry."

Wow. A guy approximately my own age who was actually a gentleman. My shoulder muscles uncoiled slightly. Clearly I had been right about Whit from the beginning, even though my original judgment had been made in the midst of an alcohol blitz. This was a genuinely nice guy. I couldn't take Natasha's evilness out on him.

"It's okay," I said.

"No. It's not. I—"

"Really, Whittaker," I said. "I was there too. I knew what I was doing." At least I thought I knew. Until last night, when I found out what it actually looked like. "It's not all on you."

Whittaker smiled his thanks. "Still, you are a lady. You deserve to be treated like one."

Oh, I am *so* not a lady.

"Thank you," I said, trying to smile.

"So," he said, then laughed. "Now that the awkward part is over, shall we agree to be . . . friends?"

Friends? Yes. Oh, thank you. Thank you, thank you, thank you.

"Sure," I said.

"Good. Friends it is," Whittaker said. Then he caught my hand in his, lifted it, and kissed it lightly.

Right. None of my other friends did that, but okay.

"I have a meeting with the dean now, but I'll see you at dinner?" he asked, raising his eyebrows.

"See ya then," I replied.

As he turned and strolled away, I wondered if he was telling the truth about this friends thing, but I decided not to dwell on it. I had too many other things to dwell on. For now, I'd take the gentleman at his word. And later, if need be, I'd hold him to it.

skeletons

The more people the police interviewed, the more the Easton Academy rumor mill took on a life of its own. If Leanne's expulsion had been an eight, then Thomas's disappearance was a ten-plus. Everywhere I went, everyone was asking everyone else what they knew, what they'd heard—and yet, no one seemed to know anything. It was all very frustrating. The longer we all went without a clue, the more panicked the vibe became, until I felt as if the kinetic energy of the student body might actually cause a nuclear meltdown.

"So, have you heard anything?" Constance asked me, sliding into the seat next to mine in trig class, our last of the day.

"No. You?" I asked.

"I heard they kept Dash McCafferty in there for over an hour," Constance said breathlessly. "And apparently Taylor Bell came out in tears."

"What? No," I said. "Why would Taylor be crying?"

"Who knows?" Constance said. "Maybe she has a secret crush on Thomas or something."

Taylor? Not possible. Or was it? I had never seen her look twice at Thomas, and that was hard to keep from doing. More likely she had just gotten overwrought by the whole situation. Or someone had just made this whole crying thing up.

I remembered Noelle's theory and wondered if Thomas really was out there having a big laugh at the drama he was causing. Was that the real reason he hadn't told anyone where he was going? I wished for the ten millionth time that I could just see him, just ask him what the hell he was thinking. But there was a way. If I could just find out more about this Legacy thing and score an invite, I might have a chance to finally, *finally* track him down.

"Hey, let me ask you a question. Do you know anything about this thing called the Legacy?" I asked.

Constance snorted derisively and sank down in her seat. "Yeah. It's pretty much all anyone can talk about. Besides you, of course."

"Right. What is it?" I asked.

"It's some huge party in the city or something," Constance said. "It's all very hush-hush. At least from people like us."

I blinked. "People like us?" Other than our both being sophomores, Constance and I had pretty much zero in common.

"Non-legacies," Constance said. "Only people who come from, like, a long line of private-school people are invited. So not people like us."

Now it was my turn to sink into my seat. So *that* was what those girls had meant when they'd said they'd never see me there. "Oh. Really?"

"Yeah. Sucks, huh?" Constance said. "It sounds like it's gonna be incredible. Missy Thurber said that last year every guy who went got a platinum Rolex and every girl got a limited-edition Harry Winston necklace. I'd kill for a Harry Winston anything. My mom won't let me have any good jewelry until I'm eighteen. She thinks I'll lose it."

"Bummer," I said, my hopes of seeing Thomas slipping away before my eyes.

"But, hey, you're in Billings now, so maybe you'll get to go anyway."

"What do you mean?" I asked.

"You know. The Billings Girls get everything," Constance said, like it was so obvious. "You probably get an automatic invite or something."

I considered this theory for a moment. It wasn't a bad one, actually. Everyone at Easton knew that the Billings Girls were never left out of anything unless they chose to leave themselves out. Maybe this would be my first chance to exercise my automatic in. And see Thomas. God, I hoped so.

"Omigod! There he is!" Constance said suddenly, grabbing my arm.

My heart completely stopped. I looked out the window. "Thomas?"

"No! Walt Whittaker," Constance whispered, pulling her desk closer to mine. "I heard he was back from his trip."

Instantly, every single part of me drooped. Nice tease. I turned around and sure enough, standing in the hallway outside the classroom talking to our trig teacher, was none other than Whit himself. The Twin Cities, London and Vienna, hovered nearby, clutching their books, clearly waiting for him to finish his conversation. Apparently, whatever London was planning on using Whit for, the campaign had begun.

"You know him?" I asked.

"*Know* him? Our parents are totally old friends," Constance said, still gripping my arm. "They're the ones who actually suggested I apply here. Omigod, look at him. He is *so* hot."

Internal alarm. I sat up a bit straighter. "What?"

"Wow. He's *totally* lost weight," Constance said, all starry-eyed. "He must be working out."

Lost weight? Really? Huh. What had he been tipping the scales at before? Three bills?

"Wait a minute, wait a minute. Do you . . . *like* him?" I asked.

Constance ripped her gaze away from Whit for the first time and looked at me. She might as well have been one of those blissed-out fans in the front row at some pop concert.

"I've had a crush on him since I was about ten," she said. "Of course, he barely even knows I exist, but I—"

"What about Clint?" I asked. She did, after all, have a boyfriend back in New York.

Constance scoffed. "Omigod, if Walt Whittaker showed any interest in me at all, I would dump Clint like that." She added a finger snap to show just how quickly.

"Wow. I had no idea," I said, sliding down in my seat again.

I could hardly believe that a guy like Whit could inspire such ardor in a girl, but it just went to show there was someone for everyone. And it turned out that Constance's someone just happened to be the same someone who had stuck his tongue down my throat just a couple of nights ago.

"Oh, no one does. I keep it completely on the DL," Constance said, then gasped. "Don't tell anyone, okay?"

"Don't worry, I won't."

Just like I won't be telling you about a certain illicit encounter with a certain someone in the woods Sunday night.

Just what I needed. More secrets from more people. Pretty soon it was going to get tough keeping them all straight.

friends with benefits

Another night passed. Then another. There was no word of Thomas. Every hour of every day was occupied with either chores, class, or avoiding Natasha, which wasn't easy, considering we shared a room. I hadn't searched Noelle's room or anyone else's. Hadn't so much as opened a drawer. The longer Natasha went without mentioning it, the more I hoped she might just forget about it.

A girl could dream.

Still, all the work and worry and stealth maneuvering to avoid her took their toll. I couldn't sleep, could hardly eat, and was still waiting for the police to come talk to me. By the end of the week, I felt like a shadow of my former self.

On Friday at lunch I placed my overloaded tray at the end of the Billings table and handed out the food I had been told to procure. Then I dropped down into one of two empty seats and pulled out my trig text with a sigh. I had a quiz that afternoon. I couldn't even remember what chapter it was supposed to cover.

Listlessly, I flipped through the pages, noticing my raw, irritated fingertips, red from cleaning products and chapped from too much washing. My knuckles were cracked as well and there were little nicks and cuts all over my hands. I was truly becoming a hard laborer.

A shadow fell over my book just as I decided on a chapter to read through. Or more likely, one sentence to read through over and over and over again without absorbing a thing. Someone cleared his throat. Finally I looked up.

Whit hovered over me, his hands behind his back, a mischievous smile on his face. He wore a green sweater with a tiny hound's-tooth pattern that on him looked like way too many hound's teeth.

"Hello, Reed," he said, near giddy.

"Hi . . . ?"

I looked around at the others. A few of them watched with interest. London, who sat at the next table just behind Noelle, seemed especially intrigued. She actually stopped grooming and turned around.

"What's up?" I said.

"I have something for you," Whit told me. "Nothing big. Don't worry. I just . . . I saw them and I thought of you."

Big gulp.

"Them?" I said.

Whittaker produced a small box from behind his back. It was gray and shiny and had gold lettering. I stared at it.

Whatever was in that box, I had a feeling it was not "just friends" appropriate. In fact, no random gift on a random day would be "just friends" appropriate. This was not good.

I glanced around. A few people at adjacent tables were starting to take notice. London glared at me with obvious envy and Vienna looked, in a word, stunned. I glimpsed Constance just entering the lunch line at the back of the room. Apparently she hadn't seen.

"Go ahead. Open it," Whittaker said.

If I made a big stink about this, we would only draw more attention. And right now, the one person who *really* didn't need to see this was hidden from view.

"God, Reed, what's the hesitation?" Kiran asked. "It's *jewelry*."

"You're giving her jewelry?" Josh asked, looking annoyed.

"It's not a big deal," Whittaker said. "Just open it, Reed."

I smiled at Whittaker, embarrassed for both of us, and took the box. I quickly lifted the lid and removed the small black velvet box inside. My hands trembled as I struggled to crack it open. Finally it popped wide with a creak, startling me. The whole thing almost slipped out of my fingers, but I caught it just in time.

"Holy crap," I blurted.

Everyone laughed. Sitting against the black satin were two large, square diamonds. Earrings. More expensive than anything I had ever owned, or would ever own, in my lifetime probably. Taylor and Kiran both stood on their toes to see into the box. London and Vienna both knelt on their chairs and turned around, nearly knocking each other over to get a look.

"What the hell?" London blurted, earning an admonishing whack from Vienna. London dropped back into her chair and sulked.

"Wow. Nice choice, Whit," Kiran said. "You have a good eye."

Whittaker beamed at the praise. "I was in town for dinner with my grandmother last night and I saw them in a shop window and I just knew you had to have them," he said. "What do you think? Do you like them?"

Diamond earrings. My very own diamond earrings. All the other girls at the table had similar pairs. Whenever they wore them I tried not to stare, not to covet. But now I had my own. I had no idea what to say. Except why, why, *why* was he giving these to me?

"They're . . . they're gorgeous," I told him. Then I screwed up every ounce of strength in my soul to add, "But I can't accept them."

"Sure you can," Whittaker said, without missing a beat.

"They're too much," I said.

"Reed," Noelle said through her teeth. "Don't be rude."

I glanced around at the girls. They were all giving me the same admonishing look. Was that what I would be doing if I didn't take these earrings that probably could have paid for my entire tuition? If I got him back that money so that he wouldn't be wasting it on someone who was not now, nor would ever be, attracted to him? If I refused to lead him on, would that be rude in their world?

From the death glares I was currently fielding, apparently so.

I looked up at Whit. He looked so hopeful and happy. The last thing I wanted to do was humiliate him in front of everyone. And besides, Constance would be re-emerging from the lunch line at any second. I couldn't let her see this. Unless I wanted to crush her.

"Thank you, Whit. This was really . . . sweet of you," I said finally. I closed the box and placed it back inside the larger one.

"It was my pleasure," he said with a self-satisfied grin.

Then he glanced over my shoulder. "Oh! There's Mrs. Solerno. I haven't seen her yet. My grandmother would kill me if I didn't say hello."

Who was this grandmother? And how could I get her to stop taking him into town and letting him blow his wad on ill-advised gifts?

"I'll be right back," he said.

Then he squeezed my shoulder and walked off.

"Wow. I guess Whit really likes you," Ariana said the second he was gone.

"Good for Whit," Dash said, like a proud papa.

"Moving on already, huh, Reed?" Josh asked.

My cheeks burned and everyone fell silent for a long moment. Josh's face flushed too, as if he had just realized how hurtful his words were, and he averted his eyes.

"First of all, Hollis, Reed's personal life is none of your business," Noelle snapped. "Second, your little buddy bailed without so much as a warning. She has every right to move on."

"Sorry," Josh said. He crumpled up his napkin and threw it down. "I gotta go."

He shoved himself up from the table, shot me an apologetic look, and walked off. For some reason, I couldn't swallow for a solid minute. Everyone watched me and waited.

"Uh, hate to burst your bubble, everyone," I said finally, tremulously. "But Whittaker and I are just friends." I quickly stashed the earrings in the bottom of my bag.

"Shyah, right," Gage said, sucking on his soup spoon. "'Cause I buy all my friends five-thousand-dollar earrings for no reason."

My mind spun. Five thousand dollars. Five *thousand* dollars.

"Come on, new girl. Give the poor guy a shot," Dash wheedled, popping a few grapes into his mouth. "He deserves to get a little."

Noelle whacked his arm with the back of her hand and all the guys snickered.

"Ha ha," I said, pretending to focus again on my book. "Sorry to disappoint, but we really are just friends. It was *his* idea to be just friends."

"Uh-huh," Natasha said under her breath. Her voice gave me chills. "You just keep telling yourself that."

true colors

"Reed."

I kept walking, ducking my head into the wind. I couldn't hear her. The wind was too loud. Let her believe that I couldn't hear her.

"Reed! Reed, I know you can hear me."

I stopped walking and turned around to face Natasha. Her curls danced around her head in the wind, giving her a very Medusa look.

"I know you've been avoiding me," she said, hugging a couple of notebooks to her chest. "And I've let you because I was giving you time to do your job. So tell me. What have you found?"

"Nothing," I replied.

Her eyebrows shot up. "Nothing?"

I sighed and looked at my feet. "I've kind of had other things on my mind, Natasha," I said, trying to sound annoyed. Annoyed and unaffected and not scared. "You know . . . school, soccer, missing boyfriend?"

Take pity. Come on. You know you want to take pity.

"Weren't thinking about the missing boyfriend much when

you were crawling all over Whittaker, were you?" she said. "Thomas is on that e-mail list, too, you know. Do you want him to come back and find out what you really are?"

My face burned with anger. "And what's that?"

Natasha took a step closer to me. Her eyes were amused. "A cheating, drunken slut who's too weak to stand up and take care of herself. Maybe he'd like to know about those little baubles in your bag as well. Accepting gifts from another guy," she said, clucking her tongue. "Yeah. You sure are the faithful, concerned girlfriend."

I could have hit her. I could have smacked her right then and there. And I might have, if several teachers and police officers hadn't been milling around the quad at that very moment.

"You don't owe them anything, Reed," Natasha said. "Do what's right. Or you know what I'm going to have to do."

She turned and strolled off, carefree, as if we'd been discussing the weather. When I turned around, I was face-to-face with Josh. My hand flew to my chest. I really didn't think I could take much more of this.

"Sorry," he said, adjusting the strap on his backpack. "I scared you."

"It's fine," I said, pushing past him. I didn't have any room for more of his jabs.

"Reed! Can I just apologize?" he asked.

I stopped and blew out a breath. Then I turned to face him.

"What the hell was that?" I demanded.

He looked almost desperate as he stepped toward me. "I don't know. I'm sorry. It just came out."

"Well, Noelle was right. It's really none of your business what I do," I told him.

"Reed, come on. Don't say that," he said.

"Why not?" I asked.

"Because. I was hoping we could be . . . I don't know . . . friends," he said, lifting his shoulders. "You're one of the only normal people at this school and I . . . I like you."

It was such a simple, sweet statement that I felt my tension start to ebb. "You do?"

Josh smiled. He had a perfect, boyish smile. "Yeah. I do."

"Then why did you say that?" I asked him. "It kind of stung, you know."

"I know. I'm sorry. I can be judgmental sometimes. It's a flaw," he said. "I *will* work on it, though. If you'll forgive me."

Somehow, I found myself grinning. "Okay, fine. You're forgiven."

"Really? Thank you. I really am sorry—"

I held up a hand. "Let's just not talk about it anymore, okay?"

"Fair enough. Well, better get to class."

Right. Class. Somehow that supposedly important aspect of being here at Easton had dropped fairly low on my priority list.

"See you later?" he asked.

"Definitely," I replied.

Then I turned and walked off smiling toward my class building. Unbelievable. In two seconds Josh Hollis had actually almost made me forget entirely about Natasha's threats.

Almost.

accusation

My foot bounced up and down under my desk as I sat in trig class before the bell, trying to cram in some last-minute information. I shot a pathetic smile at Constance as she dropped into the seat next to mine.

"Ready for the quiz?" I asked.

"Yeah. So I have a question." Her voice was unnaturally high-pitched. She laced her fingers together on her desk as she turned to me. "Why is Walt Whittaker giving you gifts?"

My stomach turned. This was not what I needed right now.

"You saw that?" I asked, rubbing at a sudden headache that had just sprung up between my eyes.

"*No*. Missy and Lorna did," she replied. "I don't believe this. Yesterday I'm pouring my heart out to you about my *feelings for him*," she said under her breath. "And the whole time you two have a thing going on. I'm such an idiot."

"No, Constance. It is *so* not like that," I said. "We do not have a thing going on. There is no thing."

"Yeah, right," she said. "Wonder what Thomas would say if he knew about this."

I swallowed against a dry throat. People around here really did know how to hit a girl where it hurt.

"Nothing. He would say nothing because it's nothing." I took a deep breath as Constance stared resolutely at the blackboard. Around us our classmates steadily filled in the empty seats. "Look, Whit may have a tiny crush on me, but that's it. And he's gonna get over it really fast because I swear I have *no* feelings for him."

How could I when this thing with Thomas was still so unresolved? I thought of Josh's accusation in the cafeteria and my insides squirmed.

But then I realized how all this looked. They had no idea that all I wanted was to see Thomas again so that I could make sure he was all right, so that I could get a little closure. How could I blame them for thinking the worst of me?

Constance sighed and glanced at me out of the corner of her eye. "You swear?"

"I swear," I said.

The ramrod-straight posture she'd been working since beginning her tirade relaxed slightly and she leaned back in her seat. Outside the door I saw our trig professor, Mr. Crandle, chatting with another teacher.

"Listen, if you like him so much, you should talk to him," I whispered. "Maybe you guys can get together."

Constance's cheeks turned pink and she looked down at her

polished nails. Under her desk, she crossed her legs demurely at the ankles.

"He doesn't even know I exist," she said.

"I doubt that's true. Whit doesn't seem like the kind of guy who'd forget an old family friend," I said.

"Maybe," Constance said, biting her lip. "I don't know. But what if he doesn't remember me? I'd feel like such a moron." Suddenly her entire face lit up and she lifted her head. "Wait! Maybe *you* could talk to him for me. Mention me and see what he says?"

She was too cute. Really. So cute it almost made me want to wrap her up in a pink bow and stick her in a cat carrier.

"Sure," I told her. "I can do that."

"Really?" she squealed, reaching over to grab my hand. "That would be *so* amazing."

Not really. Because if I talked up Constance to Whittaker and he ended up going for her then it would exponentially benefit me. The Billings Girls might be disappointed that I didn't land the guy who could "give me things," but they couldn't fault me if he fell for someone else. Plus Whit would be happy, and then I wouldn't have to hang out with him so much and constantly be reminded of those disgusting pictures. I would be able to concentrate on what really mattered—namely, figuring out what to do about Natasha, keeping my ass in school, and finding out how to get to this Legacy thing so I could see Thomas. It was win, win, win, really. For me, Whittaker, *and* Constance.

"It's not a problem," I told her, adopting a benevolent smile.

"Thank you *so* much."

Just then Mr. Crandle walked in, the other teacher trailing behind him. I hadn't seen this guy around before and as whispers started to run rampant around the room, my heart started to pound with fear.

This was no teacher.

"Miss Brennan, this is Detective Hauer," Mr. Crandle said. "He'd like to speak to you. Please gather your things and go with him."

Everyone turned to gape at me as if we hadn't all known this was coming. My hands trembled as I reached for my books. I glanced at Detective Hauer, a short, stocky man in a wrinkled shirt and cotton tie who stood at the front of the room with his hands behind his back, his razor-sharp brown eyes watching my every move.

Guilty. That was how I felt under his gaze. Guilty. But of what? Of finding a note from my ex-boyfriend? Smack on the shackles and take me to the guillotine.

I managed to rise out of my seat without my knees knocking together too much and joined the detective.

"Hello, Reed," he said. His voice was so deep it made my bones rumble.

"Hello."

I even *sounded* guilty.

He raised a hand to usher me out of the room ahead of him.

"You can make up the quiz tomorrow, Miss Brennan," Mr. Crandle said helpfully as I reached the door.

Right. Because that was what I was really concerned about.

denial

Just tell them.

No, don't. Thomas will be so mad.

So what? You're already mad at him. Besides, it's the law. Can they arrest me for not telling?

Don't do it. His parents will be on him like peanut butter on jelly. It's a betrayal.

But didn't he betray me by breaking up with me in a note?

Just do it.

Don't.

Come on.

No.

No, no, no.

"You know, there's nothing to be nervous about, Reed," Detective Hauer said.

I stopped chewing on the end of the hood string on my sweat-shirt and sat up. "I'm not nervous."

Yeah. That was very convincing. The high octave and the spittle were especially compelling.

"Would you like something to drink?" he asked.

"No, thanks. I'm fine."

I smiled at the detective, who sat behind Dean Marcus's wide desk. Then I flashed the same grin at Chief Sheridan, who hovered in the corner near one of the sky-high bookshelves. Behind me, in a cushy chair, was my advisor, Ms. Naylor. Apparently she was there to act as a student advocate, which meant, I supposed, that if they tried to beat me with a telephone book, she was required to ask them politely to stop.

Whether or not she would actually do that was another story. I never got the impression that Ms. Naylor relished my presence at Easton that much or her involvement in my life.

"So, we understand you and Mr. Pearson have been dating," the detective said, glancing at a piece of paper in front of him.

"Yes." I sat up a little straighter, trying to see what the paper had to say.

"For how long?" the detective asked. He pulled the page closer to him. The chief shifted, bringing one arm across his stomach and resting his other elbow on it, hand under chin.

"Since the third week of school," I said, endeavoring to swallow. "So not long at all."

"I see," the detective said. "Is it serious?"

I cleared my throat. "Depends on your definition of serious."

The detective smiled indulgently. "How well do you know him?"

"Pretty well, I guess," I said. "But then, everybody has secrets, right?"

His eyebrows popped up. "Do they?"

Oh, God. Why did I say that? Why, why, why?

"Did Thomas share any secrets with you, Miss Brennan?" he asked. "Where he might be going, for example?"

Yes. Yes, he did. He did, did, did.

"No," I said. "No, he didn't."

The detective eyed me as if he was trying to see inside my brain. It made me feel all hot and prickly. He looked down again.

"Is it true that last week the two of you fought outside the cafeteria?"

My face heated up like a black slate in the sun. "How did you—"

"Several witnesses have mentioned it," the detective said.

Nice. Real nice. Had everyone in school come in here and pointed their fingers directly at me?

"Yes, we fought," I said.

"About what?"

About the fact that he's a drug dealer and he supplies the whole school.

"Uh . . . I'd rather not say," I replied.

Both the chief and Detective Hauer blinked in the exact same incredulous way. So they'd never heard of an evasive teenager before?

"We'd rather you did, Miss Brennan," the chief said, speaking for the first time. "All we're trying to do here is find out where Thomas might have gone. Sometimes people miss the significance of small things. We're just trying to discern whether you happen to know something that might help us. That's all."

"Oh. Okay. Well, I . . . I found out he was lying to me," I said.

"About what?"

"He told me that he'd told his parents about me, but I found out that he hadn't," I said. Not a total fabrication. I *had* found that out as well, just days later. "So I was angry. We broke up."

"You did?" the detective said, raising his eyebrows.

"Yes. But then we got back together," I said. "You know how it is."

I giggled. The detective rubbed his temples and blew out a sigh. I sounded flighty. Flighty and stupid and nervous.

"When did you get back together?" the detective asked finally, making a note on his paper.

"Friday morning," I said definitively.

Confidence, Reed. This wasn't so bad. I could answer their questions. I had nothing to hide.

"Friday morning?"

They seemed very intrigued by this fact.

"Yes."

"So the morning of the day that Thomas disappeared," the detective said.

I cleared my throat. *Why did I clear my throat?* "Sorry," I said, coughing. "Yes."

"When did you last see Mr. Pearson?" the detective asked.

"Then. I mean, that morning. In my—"

No. Can't say that. Can't have boys in the dorm room, stupid. Say that and you get thrown out of school before you can say, "Natasha Crenshaw." Ms. Naylor's eyes gouged caverns in the back of my skull.

"That is, *behind* my dorm. Bradwell," I told them. "Before

breakfast. But I don't live there anymore. In Bradwell, I mean. I live in Billings now. In case you need to know for your . . . whatever."

Shut up! Shut up, shut up, shut up!

"And you didn't see him for the rest of the day," they said.

I cleared my throat again. Apparently I was becoming my grandfather. "No. I tried to call him a few times, but I kept getting his voice mail."

"Miss Brennan, has Thomas Pearson contacted you in any way since you last saw him?" the detective asked.

Well. There it was. He'd finally gotten to it.

"Miss Brennan? *Has* Thomas Pearson contacted you?"

Yes, he has.

No, he hasn't.

Yes. He has.

"No," I replied.

"You haven't heard from him at all."

Well, not technically. You haven't heard anything. You've read something, but you haven't heard anything.

"Reed?"

"No. I haven't," I said.

Could they get a search warrant for a minor's dorm room? Maybe they didn't even need one. Maybe they were searching it right now. Maybe they were just keeping me here while their goon squad tossed my stuff. I had to burn the note. I had to get back and burn the note now.

"I haven't."

The detective and the chief stared at me for a long, long moment. Long enough for me to remember Ariana's advice that I should be prepared for this, that I should know what I was going to say. Long enough for me to start to sweat. Long enough to imagine what it might feel like to be loaded into the back of a police cruiser and taken downtown for further questioning.

Was this the reason for her warning? Was she just trying to make this experience easier on me? Maybe she didn't suspect me of anything. Maybe she was just trying to be nice.

Damn. Why didn't I listen to her?

"You're sure."

"I haven't."

They were the only two words I could think or say.

I haven't. I haven't, I haven't, I haven't. If I made myself believe it, maybe they would too.

"Okay, then, Miss Brennan," the chief said finally. "Thank you for your time."

model friend

When I walked out of the office I felt hollow. I felt like I had been used up, wrung dry, and tossed aside. I felt like I needed a nap. I shut the door behind me, leaned back against the cool brick wall, and let out a breath. I looked up at the ceiling, where a frosted-glass light fixture hummed.

Dear God, please let Thomas come back soon. Or call someone. Anything. I just want this to be over.

"You okay?"

Kiran stood up from the wooden bench directly across the hall, unfolding her long legs and snapping her compact closed. Her makeup was freshly applied, with a new coat of shimmering lip balm and ten miles of lengthening mascara. As always, she looked as if she'd just stepped off a runway in Milan, whereas I probably looked like I'd just been run over by a jumbo jet on a whole different kind of runway. In Detroit.

"What are you doing here?" I asked, my heart in my throat. I had thought I was alone.

She looked at me as if I had just suggested she switch to Cover Girl. "I wanted to see if you were okay. God. Sorry for the intrusion."

"You wanted to see if *I* was okay?" I asked, stupefied.

"Yes. I heard you were next up on the list and I thought, you know, that this might be . . . difficult for you," she said, almost reluctantly. "But if you want to be alone . . ."

She flicked her bangs away from her eyes and turned down the hall. I stopped her with a hand on her arm. The velvet of her jacket was so soft I instantly withdrew, afraid I might damage it.

"No. That's okay," I said. "Thanks for coming."

Of all the Billings Girls, I would have thought Kiran would be the last one to publicly display any kind of affection. For me, anyway.

She looked me up and down and flashed a hint of a smile. "No problem. Come on. Before Naylor catches me outside of class. Woman has been trying to snag me all year."

Together we speed-walked down the hall and into the back stairwell. The very same stairwell I had raced through on the night she and her friends had ordered me to steal them a physics test from one of the downstairs offices.

The good old days. I had been so stressed out about that particular task I had almost lost it. Now I would have stolen a test every night if all this other crap would have just gone away.

Kiran led me down to the ground floor and pushed open the exit doors to the back of the building.

"Do you have to go back to class?" she asked me, slipping on her Gucci shades.

"No, they said I could spend the rest of the day in the library," I said, taking out my yellow pass.

"Good," Kiran said with a nod.

She started off along the winding path that led to the library. I had about a dozen questions for her. Like how she had found out my name was up and how she had gotten out of class. What she meant when she'd said Naylor had been trying to snag her all year. But I didn't ask any of them.

"So, how did it go?" Kiran asked, looking straight ahead. She crossed her arms over her chest and held herself tightly as she walked. Her high-heeled boots click-clacked against the flagstone path.

"It was okay. Nerve-wracking," I said.

"Why?"

"I don't know. You did it already, right?" I said.

She nodded.

"Don't you hate the way they look at you? Like you're guilty of something?"

"They didn't look at me that way," Kiran said.

Oh. That made me feel so much better.

"Besides, it's not like it was the first time I've ever been interviewed by police," she said in a bored tone.

"Really?"

"I've had stalkers," she told me matter-of-factly. "They're always asking *me* questions, as if I did something to provoke it.

As if it's my fault these psychos spend hours in front of their computers violating themselves to my picture."

All right then.

"What did they ask you?" she said.

I took a deep breath and tried to erase the mental image of some fat, balding guy in a wife-beater sitting in front of a glowing screen. . . .

Ugh. Mental note: Never be famous.

"Probably the same stuff they asked you and everyone else," I replied.

"I doubt it," Kiran said with a laugh. Then, noticing my surprised glance, she added, "You're the girlfriend."

"I guess. I don't know," I said, trudging along, kicking at fallen leaves. "They asked me what my relationship status with Thomas was, when was the last time I saw him . . ."

"And what did you say?"

"The truth," I told her. "That I saw him on Friday morning."

"And that's it?" she asked. "I mean, I'm just curious."

"Well, they also asked if I'd heard from him, of course," I said, wanting to flinch even now.

"Right . . . ," she said.

"And I told them I haven't," I said. She glanced at me out of the corner of her eye, like, *Yeah, right.* "Well, I haven't!" I said. "Why is that so hard for everyone to believe?"

Are you all psychic?

"Probably because if he'd gotten in touch with anyone, it would have been you," Kiran said flatly. "Thomas is notorious for making his girlfriends the primary relationships in his life. He's a totally whipped boy. Like, with anyone and everyone he decides to date."

"Girlfriends?"

Kiran tucked her chin and looked at me over the top of her sunglasses. "Please. You thought you were the first? What Greyhound bus did you fall off of?"

Wha—who? Had I met them? Were they here at Easton? Who *were* they? "No," I said, and scoffed. "It's just . . . he didn't have that problem with me, that's all."

"So you think," Kiran said.

We arrived at the library door. Kiran paused and took off her sunglasses. She looked at me with those stunning eyes and I actually felt honored that she deigned to train them on me.

"Listen, don't worry about the police," she said. "At least it's over. You told them everything you know and now you don't have to worry about it anymore."

I felt comforted for a split second, probably because Kiran was bothering to try to comfort me. That gesture in and of itself made me feel better. Maybe we were actually becoming friends. But what she didn't know was that I hadn't told the police everything. Not remotely.

"I mean, it's not like you *did* anything," she added.

"Thanks," I said. "Really. Thanks for coming to meet me."

Kiran clucked her tongue. "Don't do that. I don't *do* sappy."

I smirked. "Got it."

Kiran slipped her sunglasses back on, whipped open the library door, and slipped into the comforting, musty silence ahead of me.

"*Love* the library," she said sarcastically.

"Yeah," I replied with a scoff.

Personally, I was looking forward to the next hour of peace and quiet more than I'd looked forward to anything else all year.

the perfect weapon

After Kiran's surprising gesture, I realized there was no way I could spy on her and the other girls. No way in hell. These were my friends we were talking about here. Natasha had to understand that. She just had to.

After another round of chores, I trudged back to my room, determined to put an end to the insanity. I paused in front of my dorm-room door and took a deep breath. I could hear Natasha moving around inside. This was it. I was just going to have to tell her to forget it. I'd just have to appeal to her conscience. She had to have one in there somewhere, or she wouldn't care so much about Leanne—about bringing wrongdoers to justice. I had to make her see that what she was doing to me was just as wrong as what she thought Noelle and her friends had done to Leanne.

It had to work.

"You have to open the door in order to go through it, new girl," Cheyenne said, startling me as she came around the corner. "Unless you've got some superpowers you haven't made us all aware of."

I shot her a scathing look and walked into my room. Natasha's bed was covered with desk supplies, pens in one pile, Post-its in another, paper clips in another. She stood up, pulling various pads and notebooks out of the bottom desk drawer and tossing them near her pillows. Apparently she was reorganizing.

"Good. You're here," she said. "What's the status report?"

"Status report?"

"On our little project," Natasha said impatiently. "Or did our earlier conversation not get through to you? Because I can show you the slide show again right now if you need a refresher." She started for her laptop, which was also on the bed.

Okay. So much for her conscience.

"No. That's not necessary," I said grumpily.

I hefted my book bag over my head and tossed it on my own unmade bed. The socks I'd worn to bed last night lay crumpled and dirty on the floor, and soda cans littered my desk. One thing the fairy tale never talked about was Cinderella having the messiest room in the house.

"So? I know you've been cleaning ever since dinner," Natasha said, crossing her arms over her Easton sweatshirt. "Anything?"

This was not going to be pretty. "No."

Her eyes widened like a doll's. "Nothing? Reed, I'm starting to think you're not one hundred percent invested in this project."

"Natasha, these are my friends," I said, feeling desperate. "I don't want to do this."

Natasha blinked. For a second I thought I had thrown her. "Well . . . you *have* to," she said, sounding like a petulant five-year-old.

Well. If that was her strongest argument I was home free.

"Isn't there some other way for you to deal with this?" I asked.

Natasha stepped to the center of the room and looked me in the eye. "You don't get it, do you? It's not like I can go up to them and *ask* them to confess. I say one word and they're going to take whatever loose ends they might still have out there and tie them right up. They're impenetrable unless we can take them by surprise. About the only weakness they have is their overconfidence. They would never even *think* that you would go behind their backs, which is why you're the perfect weapon."

I stared at Natasha. She had really thought this through. Very thorough. And also very psychotic.

"No. If I'm going to confront them, I need proof," Natasha said. "And I can't get proof without you."

"Natasha—"

"Do I need to remind you of where you'll end up if you get kicked out of here?" she asked.

Everything inside of me stopped. "What do you mean?"

"I looked up your hometown on the Internet," she said. "Very quaint. It has its own chamber of commerce and everything. Were you guys just *so* psyched when they opened the new Blimpie last year?"

My fingers automatically curled into fists.

"Apparently you have a community college there too," Natasha said. "I bet people really go places with *that* degree."

"You are seriously deranged," I said through my teeth.

"Wrong again," Natasha said. "I'm the sane one around here. It's Noelle and her satellites who are deranged. Maybe if you did what I told you to do, you'd start figuring that out." She turned and went back to her bed, flipping open her laptop. "Or, I could just send this little e-mail. . . ."

"No!" I blurted. Natasha paused, her fingers hovering over the keys. "Don't," I said, resigned. "Fine. I'll do it. But I don't think I'm going to find anything."

Natasha closed her laptop with a click. "Sure you don't, honey," she said condescendingly. "Sure you don't."

the padded cell

The next morning I got up before the sun had even sent a wisp of light over the hills that surrounded Easton. It wasn't as if lying there wide awake, as I had all night, was doing me any good. All I had done was stare at the wall and imagine myself getting caught by Noelle, Ariana, Kiran, and Taylor in a million different ways. I pictured what they would do, how they would react. In one version Noelle took out a bat and whacked me across the head, showering her bestest friends with blood and brains. But I think I had been drifting off when that one occurred, so it was a half-dream. Whatever the case, it had kept me awake for the next three hours.

So I got up, made my own bed, straightened my stuff, and took a shower. Natasha tossed and turned and huffed whenever I made a noise above a whisper, but she said nothing. Good thing. I was, after all, doing this all for her.

And for myself. And my future.

Soon everyone started to stir and I was able to vacuum. Some girls said good morning to me on their way downstairs; others didn't bother. I didn't care much. All I could think about was what I was about to do.

I was hovering in the shadows at the end of the hallway when Kiran and Taylor walked out together, debating whether travel within the contiguous United States was even worth the time it took to pack a bag. (Taylor was pro, Kiran was con.) Shaking like I was about to meet my executioner, I waited until they rounded the corner, then sprang forward and slipped into their room. The second I was inside, I realized there was no need for the cloak-and-dagger act. I was supposed to be here. There were the unmade beds, the piles of laundry, the musty bathroom. I could have walked in here while they were still getting dressed and it would have been fine. Expected, even. Way to stress myself out.

Relaxing ever so slightly, I got to work on the beds. I'd do the chores first and get them over with, then snoop around a little. That way if I had to leave suddenly, my work would be done when I bailed. After making sure everything was in order, I stood in the center of the room and looked around. Where to begin?

My eyes fell on Kiran's closet. Might as well start with my favorite place in the room. I walked over and placed my hands on the two knobs that worked the sliding doors. I listened for noises. Someone was showering in another room, but that was all I could hear. I steeled myself—I was doing this for a reason, I was doing this because I had to—and threw the doors open.

Right. Don't get distracted by the thousands upon thousands of dollars' worth of designer clothes. You want to get this over with.

Shoe boxes lined the floor, stacked three boxes high and at least twelve across. I dropped to my knees and opened the first box. Black stilettos. The one under it, suede camel sling backs. The one under that, red kitten-heeled sandals. God, a girl could go crazy in here.

Focus. Your future or trying on a pair of shoes?

I opted for a future. One by one I went through all the boxes and found nothing but shoes, shoes, and more shoes. Then on the far end, the purses began. I worked my way up through shelves of clutches and hobos and shoppers and minis to the shelves of sweaters above the hanging rod. Already I was sweating. This could take forever.

I dragged Taylor's desk chair over and stood up on it, moving the first stack of sweaters aside carefully so that they would appear untouched. My eyes fell on something out of place. It was a huge, black-and-white NO!

Well. That was incriminating enough. Tenderly I took down two stacks of sweaters and laid them reverently on Kiran's bed. I stepped back up on the chair to have a better look. There, shoved into the farthest, darkest corner of Kiran's closet, was a brown box with a small padlock and magazine clippings pasted all over it. Like something out of a serial killer's house.

NO!

STAY AWAY

DON'T TOUCH

Itching with curiosity, I reached for the box and pulled it toward me. It was heavy and made of wood. Among the words and hastily assembled letters were clippings of pictures of farm animals. Pigs and cows, mostly. What the hell *was* this thing?

I reached for the lock, expecting it to be, of course, locked, but it fell right open. My heart skipped a beat. I removed the lock and slowly opened the box. The first thing I noticed was the picture of some poor woman's humongous, cellulite-ridden ass in a flowered bathing suit taped up inside the box top. The second was the smell of icing.

Oh. My. God.

The box was full of snacks. Hostess cupcakes, Twinkies, Oreos, Ding Dongs, Nutter Butters, brownies, coffee cakes, SnoBalls, Milanos. It was sick. If she was so worried about eating it, why go to all the trouble of creating a box to keep it in—a box designed to keep her away? Was it some kind of torture?

I noticed a small, spiral-bound notebook propped flat against the side of the box and moved some Devil Dogs aside to pull it out. Inside was an entry marked September 9. Beneath it was a list of every single thing Kiran had eaten that day and the calorie content of that item. At the bottom was written "Twenty Oreos," and next to it, in a psychotic scrawl, the words "No, No, No!"

I covered my mouth with my hand. This poor girl. This poor, *poor* girl. Talk about an eating disorder; this was more like an infectious disease. Kiran was seriously struggling.

I turned the page in the notebook. The following day there was no sugar intake and a smiling face was drawn at the bottom. But every day after that there were more snacks and more crazy admonishments.

Turned out Kiran was not as flawless as she would have the world believe. From her cool demeanor and the casual way she chose her food at meals, I never would have known. As badly as I felt for her, I can't say it wasn't good to know. Comforting, in a way, to know someone that perfect didn't actually exist. But, of course, this had nothing to do with Leanne.

Reluctantly, I shoved the food diary back where I'd found it and replaced all Kiran's things. The closet search had turned up nothing to help Natasha's case.

Was this a good thing or a bad thing?

I had a few more minutes, so I decided to check under Taylor's bed. I yanked out a few under-the-bed boxes full of notebooks and texts. When I pulled one of them out, a sheaf of printer paper exploded all over the room, white sheets flying everywhere.

"Oh, crap," I said under my breath, gathering them up. They must have been piled loosely atop one of the boxes. There was no way I was ever going to get them back in the right order.

Please let them be numbered. Please, please, please.

But as I stacked the pages back up, I realized it didn't matter if they were numbered. Each and every page was filled with exactly the same thing—the same phrase typed over and over and over again:

I am good enough. I am good enough. I am good enough. I am good enough.

I snorted a surprised laugh. I couldn't help it. But then I instantly felt guilty. Taylor was losing it, clearly. Of course, I supposed all geniuses were a little off. But this was ridiculous.

Fifty pages, at least, of *this*? She was the smartest girl ever to walk the halls of Easton. I couldn't believe she needed all this affirmation. When did she have time to sit down and *do* this?

Hidden snack cakes and obsessive affirmations. No wonder these two were roommates. Did each know what the other was hiding? Maybe if they did they could help each other.

"Taylor! Hurry up!" someone shouted from downstairs.

There were footsteps on the stairs.

"I just have to get my planner!" Taylor called back. She was right down the hall.

Shaking violently, I shoved the papers back on top of the box and pushed it under the bed. Then the second, then the third. The third got caught on the leg of the bed and I was just jimmying it back into place when the door flew open. I stood up, straightened my sweater and looked right into Taylor's surprised eyes.

"Reed! God! You scared me," she said, then glanced at her bed.

"Sorry. I was just finishing up in here," I said.

"Oh. Okay," she said, stepping uncertainly toward me. It was almost as if she knew what I had found. She grabbed her PDA off the nightstand and smiled. "Come on. Let's . . . go to breakfast."

"Okay," I said. "Let me just grab my book bag."

"Oh, hey. Reed?" she said, pausing as she stepped into the hall. She fumbled with her bag and pulled out a neatly typed paper in a light blue cover. "You're good with the classic writers, right?"

I closed the door behind me. "Yeah."

"Well, I was wondering if you could read this paper over for me," she said, handing it to me. "I know I'm a year ahead and

KATE BRIAN

116

everything, but it needs another eye before I hand it in. I just want to be sure it's . . . you know . . . good enough."

Good enough. Good enough, good enough, good enough.

Oh, my God.

"I'm sure it's great," I told her firmly. "Everyone's always saying you're the smartest person ever to even go here."

"That's what *they* think." Taylor managed a wan smile. "Still, I could use your help."

"Oh. Definitely. I'll read it today," I said, backing away.

"Where're you going?" she asked.

"To my room. To get my bag, remember?" I said.

"Oh. Right. Okay. See you downstairs!" Taylor said brightly. "And Reed? Thanks."

"No problem."

I jogged back to the safety of my own room, closed the door behind me, and looked at the paper. Poor Taylor. She thought she needed a sophomore to tell her that her paper was good? And Kiran! Who knew it was possible that these paramours of perfection could be hiding such secrets?

The other girls in this school would kill for information like this. Unfortunately, there was one person who couldn't have cared less: Natasha. There was only one bit of info she was looking for and I hadn't found it. Yet.

matchmaker

Saturday was a gorgeous fall day, with a crisp wind and a sky so blue it looked fake. A perfect day for soccer. A perfect day for taking out days of pent-up aggression on unsuspecting Barton School girls. Orange, brown, and yellow leaves danced their crackly dance across the dewy grass as Josh, Noelle, Kiran, Taylor, and I made our way to the visitors' parking lot, where several buses were parked, waiting to whisk us to Barton for our away games. Taylor and Kiran both played field hockey and their game would be on the field adjacent to ours. Basically, it was going to be mayhem—whistles, shouts, and crunching bones. I was very much looking forward to it.

"God, I could just go to sleep right now," Josh said, stretching his arms above his head. "I think I ate too many pancakes this morning. They put me right out."

"Wow. You're gonna be really useful on the soccer field today," I teased.

Josh, like me, played defense—on the men's team, of course.

"I don't know how you can eat those things," Kiran said,

crossing her arms over her stomach as we rounded a bend under a tunnel of colorful leaves. "That's enough calories for a whole week right there."

"Like you've ever eaten enough calories for a whole week. Even *in* a whole week," Noelle joked.

"Hey! I eat! I do! You've seen me eat," Kiran replied, suddenly manic. "You've seen me eat, right, Reed?"

"Uh . . . yeah," I said. Because I had. Until I'd found that psycho box I never would have known Kiran had issues. "Of course you eat. And you look perfect, by the way."

A little affirmation couldn't hurt, right?

"See?" Kiran said triumphantly. "Reed's seen me eat."

"Okay! Okay! Calm down already before you give yourself the shakes," Noelle said.

"I vote for a change of topic!" Taylor put in, casting Kiran a worried look. So maybe she *did* know what went on in her roommate's closet.

"Fine. Reed, how's it going with Whittaker?" Noelle asked.

I glanced warily at Josh, who instantly became very interested in the nearest tree.

"How's what going?"

"Has he asked you to *go steady* yet?" Kiran said sarcastically, causing Taylor to snort a laugh.

"Yeah. Did he *pin* you?" Taylor asked.

"He does sort of seem like he's out of another era, doesn't he?" I said. "Like we should all be wearing poodle skirts and super-high ponytails."

"I think it's sweet," Noelle said. "At least he's a gentleman."

Kiran, Taylor, Josh, and I all paused. Noelle stopped a few feet ahead and turned with an exasperated sigh. "Problem?"

"Uh, yeah. You just complimented someone with no trace of sarcasm or malice," Kiran said.

"Not just someone. Walt Whittaker," Taylor pointed out.

"Are you self-medicating again?" Kiran asked.

"Kiran, you're a model. Don't try to be funny," Noelle said, earning a laugh from Josh. "And, news alert, I set Reed up with the guy. That means it's my responsibility not to mock him until *after* they've gone horizontal."

Ugh. We all had to groan at that one.

"We are not going to be . . . you know . . . doing that," I told them in no uncertain terms. "We're *just friends.*"

"You're sure about that," Noelle said, taking a step toward me.

I lifted my chin. She could make me vacuum her room and clean out her hair brush and shine her shoes, but she could not tell me who to date. I had to draw the line somewhere. Josh was watching me closely.

"Yes. I'm sure," I said.

"Well, you might want to tell him that," she said, turning me around and pointing. Whit was coming toward us down the path, an eager smile on his face as he bore down on me. "Because that is not the face of a person who wants to talk to a friend."

"Good morning, all," Whit said, with a slight bow of his head. "How is everyone this fine day?"

"We're all just fabulous, Whit. Thanks for asking," Noelle said, slinging her arm over Kiran's shoulder. Kiran turned and laughed into Noelle's jacket. "We'll leave you two alone, won't we?"

"Sure. 'Bye, Whit!" Taylor said. Then the three of them traipsed off, arm in arm, toward the buses, leaving me seething in Whit's shadow.

"See you guys later," Josh added before loping away.

"'Bye!" I said loudly. Like somehow that would make him come back and save me.

"Hello, Reed," Whit said huskily. "How are you?"

"Fine," I said. I turned and walked toward the end of the path. He, of course, fell into step with me. "How are you?"

"I'm well," he said, nodding. "Thank you for asking."

We had come to the edge of the parking lot. The various teams were gathered together in clumps as the bus drivers and coaches tried to sort out which bus was going where. A couple of the guys' teams were off to other schools and apparently there had been some crossed wires. I paused and let out a sigh. Looked like my hopes of getting on the bus and jetting off were dashed.

"Which sport do you play?" he asked.

"Soccer," I told him.

"A rough sport," he said. "You seem too delicate for such a rough sport."

"Well, then you don't know me," I replied, sounding a bit harsher than I intended.

Whit, however, didn't seem to notice. He just smiled at me for a long moment as if I'd said something amusing. Long enough to make me squirm. And then, gradually, his face fell.

"What?" I said.

"You're not wearing the earrings," he said.

He reached out and touched my bare earlobe, pressing it gently between his thumb and forefinger. I tilted my head and shrugged away.

This was unbelievable. Couldn't he take a hint? Maybe I should just tell him I had a boyfriend. Except that I didn't, thanks to Thomas's secret breakup note. Not that anyone other than me knew that.

God, I wished Thomas were there right then. So I could throttle him.

"No . . . they're a little much for a soccer game, don't you think?" I asked.

"But you haven't worn them since I gave them to you," he said. "Do you not like them?"

"No. It's not that," I said. "It's just . . ."

Out of the corner of my eye I saw Constance standing with the rest of the cross-country team. She was watching me—watching *us*—very closely. Surreptitiously, I turned my hand, palm out at my side, and crooked my fingers, waving her over.

"It's just, they seem more like special-occasion earrings," I told him. "They're too nice to wear every day."

Constance shook her head very slightly and shifted her feet. I crooked my fingers more insistently.

"But the man at the store said they *were* everyday earrings," Whittaker told me. "That was why I purchased them. So that you could wear them every day."

Someone behind me giggled. Damn eavesdroppers. I so didn't

like where this conversation was going, and the last thing I needed
was for anyone else to overhear it. I did the only thing I could
think to do: I sacrificed a friend.

"Constance!" I said loudly, turning my head and widening my
eyes. "Hey! I've been looking all *over* for you!"

No one had perfected the deer-in-headlights thing like
Constance. She stood there, frozen, with her eyes as wide as dinner plates. Then her head twitched and she looked at Whittaker
and her face entirely transformed. Charming smile, flirtatiously
tilted head, rosy cheeks.

"Hi, Reed," she said. "Hello, Walt."

For a moment, Whittaker seemed offended by both the interruption and the use of his first name. But then his expression
cleared and he smiled.

"Constance! Constance Talbot! My parents told me you were
matriculating here this semester! It's so good to see you!"

Constance made her way over to us. Whittaker leaned in and
gave Constance a cheek kiss, and I was almost certain she was
going to pee in her pants. The glee on her face could have warmed
the entire student body.

"Oh! You two know each other?" I said, trying my best to be the
good actress. "How great is that? Two of my favorite people and
they already know each other."

Whit looked at me quizzically.

"We were roommates at the beginning of the year," I
explained. "Constance is the best," I said, wrapping my arm
around her. She grinned at me, pleased. "Did you know she's

writing for the *Gazette*? You should tell him all about that front-page article you're working on."

Constance flushed. "No. Please. It's no big deal." She looked up at him with sheer worship in her eyes. "I'd rather hear about your trip. Was it as amazing as it sounded?"

Yes. Go, Constance. She'd hit on his favorite topic in one shot. This girl was good. Better than she gave herself credit for.

"Even more so, actually," he said. "China was absolutely awe-inspiring. When you're standing there, under the Great Wall, you really understand for the first time the capacity man has for—"

"I'm gonna let you two catch up," I said, interrupting before I got stuck. Behind Constance, I saw Noelle and some other girls from the soccer team finally boarding a bus. "Looks like they've got us sorted out."

Whittaker's brow knitted as he looked at me. "But I—"

"See ya!" I said, then turned and jogged off.

I climbed onto the bus, sat down in the first seat, and hunkered down to peek through the bottom of the window. Whittaker was still talking, gesturing hugely as he spoke, and Constance was rapt with attention. Standing out there in the sun, her in her Easton sweats and him in his trench, they looked like the perfect fresh-faced, overprivileged, prep school couple.

All I could hope was that very soon Whittaker would start seeing that too.

trunk show

Noelle Lange had sick amounts of stuff. Hundred of CDs stuffed into leather crates in her closet. A half-dozen silk boxes filled with tangled necklaces, bracelets, and earrings, most of which looked far too expensive to be treated with such carelessness. Drawers full of photographs and postcards and invitations to charity events and fashion shows. Ticket stubs from London theaters, shot glasses from exotic locales, three iPods of various sizes and colors, crystal-studded makeup cases, leather wristlets, gold and leather key chains, scented candles, digital cameras, lace thongs, manicure kits, cell phone cases. It never ended. How I would ever sort out something that mattered from all this swag that clearly didn't, I had no idea.

I stood up after closing her bottom desk drawer and blew my hair out of my face. I was almost afraid to try under the bed. What did she keep under there? Her illegal furs and bars of gold and silver?

At least I had time on my side. Noelle and Ariana were supposed to be at the library all night studying for some massive

English exam. Or, more likely, gossiping all night and trusting that their golden streak of luck and blessedness would, as always, get them through.

That golden streak was the reason I was here. All I wanted in life was to have their kind of luck. Too bad I was going to have to take them down to get it. But I couldn't think about that now. I had work to do.

Down on my hands and knees, I was about to lift Noelle's duponi comforter when I saw something out of the corner of my eye. On the floor, sticking out from behind her dresser, was a sliver of something red. Curious, I crawled over and inspected. It looked like the end of a patent leather bag. Suddenly my pulse went into overdrive. This looked like it could be something.

Bracing one hand on the front of the dresser, I reached around and yanked the bag free. It was long and slim, a plain red clutch. I leaned back against the foot of her bed and slowly unzipped it. Inside were about ten four-by-six photographs.

I pulled the first one out and almost gagged. It was Dash, and he was naked. Completely stark naked. And very . . . well . . . excited.

Barking a laugh, I slapped the photo facedown into my lap.

Oh. My. God. Was this for real? Slowly, I lifted the corner of the photo again and peeked. Yep. Still there. He was lying on his side on a double bed, his head propped up on his hand, his hairless chest cut as could be, and his penis completely erect.

Damn, was he ever endowed. This guy could totally be in porn.

Quickly, I pulled out the rest of the pictures. Dash, naked, sitting on the edge of the bed. Dash, naked, standing with a smirk on his face. Dash, naked. Dash, naked. Dash, naked. And the pièce de résistance: Dash, naked, hugging a teddy bear. Talk about blackmail. If I ever felt like taking Dash McCafferty down, I had just found the motherlode.

Shaking my head, I stuffed the photos back in their case and shoved them behind the dresser again, this time making sure no part of it was visible. No one else needed to find that. It was my good deed for the day.

I blew out a sigh and decided to try Ariana's side of the room. This time I went for the closet first and straight for the top shelf, since that was where I had uncovered Kiran's big secret. Unfortunately, Ariana's shelves contained nothing scandalous, aside from a pink crocheted sweater that I had never seen her wear and hopefully never would. Definitely one of those gifts given by a grandma that one just couldn't manage to throw away. I jumped down off the desk chair and dropped to the floor.

Tucked back toward the rear wall was an old-fashioned trunk. Huh. That definitely looked like something that might hold something scandalous. I pulled it toward me and opened the lid. Inside were piles and piles of notebooks, copies of the Easton literary magazine, various editions of *Poetry* magazine and *Writer's Weekly*, and boxes of pens and pencils. I lifted out a stack of magazines and dug through the memorabilia, looking for anything that seemed as if it didn't belong. There were random pages and scraps covered in Ariana's handwriting, drafts of poems and lines of ideas. If I'd had more time and a free pass from Ariana, I might have stopped to read some of it, but that wasn't what I was here for. Unfortunately, it looked as if I'd hit another dead end.

I was about to replace the magazines when I saw a tiny piece of brown ribbon that seemed to be lodged between the bottom of the trunk and the side. How had that gotten wedged in there? I reached in and tugged at it and my breath caught in my throat. Had the bottom of the trunk just moved?

I glanced at the outside of the trunk. Sure enough, the "floor" of the inside was about four inches higher than the bottom on the outside.

The trunk had a false bottom.

Heart pounding a mile a minute now, I dove in and took everything out. I knew this was dangerous. There was a ton of crap here and it would take me a while to replace it all. But I had to see what was in the bottom of this trunk. If Ariana was hiding something, she had done a much better job of hiding it than her friends had.

Once the trunk was clear, I grabbed the ribbon and pulled. The entire floor of the trunk pulled free. Sitting underneath it was a sleek black laptop computer.

I turned and looked over my shoulder. Ariana had a Mac all set up on her desk. What did a high school student need with a second, secret computer?

I took the computer out and rested it in my lap. I popped the top and hit the power button, just praying no one would walk in. It took the computer a few agonizing seconds to power up. What was on this thing? Was it the proof Natasha was looking for? Had Ariana and the others actually plotted to get Leanne thrown out of school? It was clear that Ariana, at least, had something worth hiding. These were pretty elaborate measures for simply stashing a laptop to keep it from getting stolen. Especially when everyone at this school could buy one of these things four thousand times over.

"Come on," I whispered. "Come on, come on. . . ."

Finally, a black screen appeared with a prompt window in the center.

"Welcome, Ariana," it read. "Password?"

And there was that white box underneath with a flashing cursor, mocking me. There would be no getting past this without a password.

Shit.

Downstairs, the front door of Billings opened and slammed. I was on my feet in an instant, carefully replacing the computer and the false bottom and all the contents of the trunk. I shoved it back into the closet, slipped out the door, and ran to the stairwell, jogging down to my own floor. It wasn't until I was back in my room that I allowed myself to breathe. I leaned back against my door and heaved, my hand over my stomach.

I was onto something. I knew I was. I had to get the password to that computer, but how? I couldn't figure out what Ariana meant half the time when she was speaking directly to me, so how was I supposed to deduce her secret password?

Didn't matter how. I had to do it. Because if there was anything to be found, it was on that computer. I was sure of it.

perfect couple

"Reed! Reed! Wait up!"

I paused on the steps to the library as Constance jogged to catch up with me. Her face was flushed and her eyes were bright with excitement. She placed her hand over her heart as she stopped in front of me to catch her breath. Just looking at her made me think of meadows in springtime and flowers blooming.

"Thank you *so much* for making me talk to Whittaker the other day," she gushed. "I never would have gone up to him on my own, but he was *so* sweet. We talked for so long Mr. Shreeber was screaming at me to get on the bus. I made us late for the meet!"

"Wow. Glad I could be of service," I said.

"He told me all about his trip to East Asia and asked me about the Cape," Constance said. "He remembered that my family goes to the Cape every summer. Not that he shouldn't. I mean, his family has visited us there a few times. But still, it was nice of him to ask, wasn't it?"

"Sure," I said, grinning as well. It was nearly impossible not to in the face of that much giddiness.

"Do you think he was flirting?" she asked me, grabbing my forearm, which was wrapped around my books.

"I—"

"Of course he wasn't flirting. Why would he flirt with me?" Constance said, pulling me aside to let a few students through to the door. "He's known me since my Elmo obsession," she said, looking at the ground.

"Your Elmo obsession?"

"Oh, I was obsessed with Elmo—you know, from *Sesame Street*?—for *way* too long. I carried that stupid doll around with me until I was, like, nine years old," Constance said. "My older brother Trey threw it in the ocean one year and Whit dove in to save it." She sighed. For the first time in my life, I saw firsthand what the expression "stars in her eyes" looked like. Kind of spooky. "I'll never forget that."

"Wow," I said. "He's a hero."

"He is, isn't he?" she asked, scrunching her nose. "Anyway, I think he might actually be interested in me. Walt Whittaker. I can't believe it. He even said we should have dinner sometime. Just me and him. To catch up on old times!"

I took a deep breath and tasted relief. "Constance, that's so great. I'm really glad it went so well."

"Me too!" she said. Then she grabbed me in both arms and hugged me. Hard. Constance was bonier than she looked.

"Come on. Let's go study!" she said.

As she dragged me through the door and into the library, I couldn't help feeling I'd finally dodged at least one bullet. If Whit and Constance started spending time together, he would have to see that she was ten times more appropriate for him than I was. And ten times more eager to be with him. And then I wouldn't have to worry about deflecting his advances or trying to remind him of our agreement to be just friends. One less thing to stress about.

I needed this. I needed it badly.

fate

When I arrived at the dinner table that night, a heated debate was taking place. Dash was definitely on one side, Noelle on the other. It was unclear as of yet whom the others had aligned themselves with. I blushed as I walked by Dash and sat down on his side of the table, as far from him as I could get, making it nearly impossible for me to see him. Ever since my illicit discovery in Noelle's room, I'd had a hard time being in the same room as Dash without constantly seeing his nether regions in my mind's eye.

Two seconds later, Josh sat down across from me. "Hey," he said.

I smiled. "Hey."

"I don't understand," Dash was saying. "One phone call and we could have a limo waiting for us anywhere in town. Do you *want* to be uncomfortable for two hours?"

"Dash, you're not getting it. This party is all about tradition," Noelle replied, gesturing with her fork. "And part of the tradition is taking the train."

They were talking about the Legacy. They had to be. The Billings Girls had never talked about it right in front of me so openly before. Were they finally, *finally* going to invite me?

"She's right, man," Gage said, leaning back on two chair legs and balancing. "The train ride is half the fun."

"Yeah. It was really fun when you booted all over the window last year on the way home and it dripped down the back of my coat," Dash said grumpily. "That was fun."

"Look. The Legacy has been going on for generations," Noelle said, taking a bite of a baby carrot. "Our forefathers took the train to the Legacy and we will take the train to the Legacy."

"Since when do you give a crap about our forefathers?" Dash asked.

"Since when are you using wax in your hair?" Noelle asked, eyeing him disdainfully.

"Oh, that's relevant," Dash replied.

God, this was torture. Didn't they realize that no one had officially told me about this thing yet? Didn't they want me to come? Talk about Cinderella. This was what she must have felt like when her annoying stepsisters kept talking about the damn ball.

Okay. Clearly I was going to have to make this opportunity for myself. Sometimes a girl had to do what a girl had to do.

"Um, I have a question," I said, leaning forward.

Everyone turned to look at me. Noelle, Kiran, Taylor, Ariana, Gage, Josh, Dash, and Natasha. It was as if they had all forgotten that I existed and my speaking was, therefore, a *complete* shock.

"What *is* the Legacy?"

Noelle and Kiran exchanged a look. Gage snorted a laugh and dropped his chair back down, reaching for a roll on his plate.

"That's for us to know and you to most likely never find out," Gage said, enjoying himself a little too much.

"Funny," I replied.

Josh cleared his throat. "He's fairly serious," he said, his expression apologetic.

I felt a blush creeping onto my cheeks. "Come on."

Dash cleared his throat and leaned onto the table to better see me. I bit the inside of my cheek to keep from laughing and tried as hard as I could not to see his guy parts superimposed over his face.

"Reed, the Legacy is an exclusive party," he said sagely. "Only private school legacies are invited."

My insides turned. I had kind of expected someone to make me an exception, to tell me they would find a way around the rule. Was it possible that Constance's theory had been completely off base?

"Not just legacies," Kiran corrected. "Multiple-generation legacies."

"Oh," I said, looking down at my food.

"'We came over on the Mayflower' legacies," Gage added.

I get it. I'm not invited. Thanks for the hammer to the head.

"The only way to get in if you're *not* a legacy is to be a legacy's plus-one," Noelle said, looking directly at Dash until he started concentrating very seriously on his food. "And only a very,

very select few even *get* a plus-one. Your family has to go back to practically the dark ages."

"Now where on Earth would Reed find a legacy with a plus-one?" Kiran pondered aloud.

I looked around at all of them, waiting for the answer, until Noelle tilted her head toward the other side of the room. I turned and followed her gaze. Whittaker. Whittaker, who was, as he always seemed to be, chatting with an adult. This time, Dean Marcus.

Suddenly it hit me like a cartoon piano to the head. This was why London had wanted to use him. This was why Vienna had suggested that every girl in school would be after him in the next few weeks. Whit could get one lucky girl into the Legacy with his coveted plus-one. If I had any shot in hell of going, I would have to be Walt Whittaker's date.

I looked at Noelle again. She arched one eyebrow and lifted a shoulder, like, *Told you so.* She had planned this from the start. The things Whittaker could get me that I wouldn't otherwise have. We weren't talking about diamond earrings or other random luxury items. We were talking about entré into exclusive parties. We were talking about acceptance among the elite. Just being a Billings Girl wasn't enough. At least not for me. I was a special case. I needed another leg up.

I took a deep breath. What Noelle didn't realize was that I couldn't be Whittaker's plus-one. I couldn't lead him on just to get an invite to some party, no matter how intriguing and mysterious and exclusive. He clearly liked me. A lot. Using him would be way too mean. And besides, Constance was totally in love with him. There was no way I was doing that to her. Except . . .

"Do you guys really think Pearson is going to be there?" Josh asked.

Except for that.

"Are you kidding? Wherever Pearson is right now, he'll be at the Legacy," Dash said. "Dude wouldn't miss this party if he was dead."

Thomas was going to be at the Legacy. His friends seemed fairly certain of that fact. That was the whole point of me trying to get to this thing, wasn't it? So that I could yell at him for everything he'd put me through. So that he could explain. So that I could see that he was okay.

Slowly, I looked up at Whittaker again. He was laughing heartily at something the dean had said—a nice, big belly laugh. And sure enough, a few random girls were looking on with stars in their eyes, just waiting to pounce on him once he was free. Thomas was going to be at this party. The only way for me to get into this party was to get Whittaker to invite me. If I wanted to see my maybe-ex, I was going to have to use my maybe-stalker to do it.

Fate had a really messed-up sense of humor.

the wrong invitation

The days had been growing rapidly shorter. Now when I left the library after a postdinner study session, the torch lights along the pathways were already aglow to light my way back to Billings. With the dark came the intensified cold. After days of resisting and coming home with my teeth chattering, I had finally caved and broken out my crappy gray wool coat with the embarrassingly short sleeves and the unidentifiable stain along the hem. Already I'd caught a few disgusted stares from the female population. I was overdue for a phone call to Dad anyway. Looked as if the next one would include me begging him to put in an order with Lands End.

Yes, Lands End. While my classmates walked around in their Prada and Coach and Miu Miu, Lands End was the best I could hope for.

I ignored a pair of girls coming in the opposite direction who stared into my semifamous face, then started twittering and talking the moment I was past them. I barely even noticed this stuff anymore. If I ever did hit it big, this semester was going to be perfect prep for handling celebrity.

I turned up the path to Billings, already mentally pep-talking myself for whatever chore list my "sisters" had devised for me, when I saw a dark figure lurking in front of the door. For the splittest of seconds I thought of Thomas and my heart caught. But then I realized that a figure of that size could belong to only one person.

"Reed," he said, stepping out of the shadows.

"Whit," I replied, mimicking his serious tone.

"How was the library?" he asked with a small, knowing smile.

I decided not to ask how he knew I'd been at the library. I'd save him the pleasure of sharing, and me the pain of hearing, how he predicted my every move.

"Fine. What's up?" I asked.

"Well, I have a question to ask you," he said, slipping his hands into the pockets of his overcoat. "An invitation to offer, actually."

The Legacy. My conscience and my desire had been at war ever since dinner the night before and neither one had yet waved the white flag. I was not prepared for this. What was I going to say? What was I going to do? Somewhere in one of the rooms above, someone was practicing the violin. Something fast and manic. It didn't help with the thinking.

"I was wondering if you would do me the honor of being my dinner guest on Friday night," he said.

Wait. His what? Where was my plus-one invite? And, hold on, he'd already asked Constance to sit with him at dinner. What was he doing, throwing out these invites like they were bath water?

"Whit, we already sit together at dinner every night," I pointed out. A stiff breeze blew past us, filling my nostrils to bursting with the pungency of his evergreen-scented aftershave. I held my breath and tried not to cough.

Whittaker chuckled. "No, no, no. Not here. Off campus," he said. "You see, Friday is my eighteenth birthday. I've been granted permission to dine off campus, and I'd like you to be my guest."

There were so many things wrong with this proposal that I didn't know where to begin.

"How did you get permission?" I said finally.

"My grandmother. She's on the board of directors and she's not above occasionally pulling the odd string," he said with pride. "She's granted you a pass as well. We don't need to bring a chaperone."

The word *chaperone* made me shudder.

"But, Whit, what about everyone else?" I said. "I mean, it's your eighteenth birthday. You don't want to spend it with just me."

His expression told me that this was exactly what he wanted. This was very not good. Clearly Whittaker was even more serious about me than I had estimated. He could be here, on campus, ringing in his eighteenth year with a drunken party in the woods with Dash and Gage and the others, but instead he wanted to whisk me to some off-campus restaurant.

"Say yes, Reed. We'll get dressed up; we'll go for a drive. I know this incredible little Italian place in Boston—"

"Boston?" I croaked. I had never been to Boston. I had never been to any city other than Philadelphia, and that was just for one day on my eighth-grade field trip.

"Of course. You didn't expect me to celebrate my eighteenth at one of the three decent restaurants here in Easton," he said with an incredulous exhale. He reached out and caught my hand in both of his, looking me deep in the eye. "Say you'll come."

My heart actually responded to that plea. He sounded so sincere, how could it not? So there I was. I could say no and crush this sweet guy and also obliterate any chance of being asked to the Legacy and seeing Thomas, or I could say yes, go to some fancy restaurant in Boston, and keep the hope of seeing Thomas alive.

In the end, it was no contest, really. My conscience took a dive.

"Okay," I said finally, nearly choking on my dry throat. "I'd love to."

pressure

My entire life I had always found brushing my teeth to be a soothing activity. It was the perfect time to ponder the events of the day in privacy. To go over the things I might have said or done differently. To pat myself on the back for the things that had gone well. Unlike the parents of every other kid on the planet, *my* parents had often been forced to yell at me to *stop* brushing my teeth. Fifteen minutes would pass while I zoned out. Half an hour. It was amazing I had any enamel left.

That night I was somewhere into my second quarter of an hour, my mouth full of foam, when the bathroom door banged open behind me. I nearly choked on my own spit.

"How's it going?" Natasha asked, folding her arms over her sizable chest and leaning against the doorjamb. She glared over my shoulder at my reflection in the mirror.

I leaned over the basin and emptied my mouth into the drain, then slowly filled the cup with water and tipped it into my mouth. After sloshing it around for a half a minute, I spit again. Let her wait. She was only waiting for nothing.

"Fine," I said finally, wiping my face with a hand towel. "I had a great day, how about you?"

"You know that's not what I'm asking," Natasha said. "What have you found?"

Let's see: a refinery's worth of sugar, evidence of serious psychological self-abuse, and some Skinamax-worthy photos. Oh, and a secret, hidden computer with a password-protect program.

I folded the towel, hung it on the towel ring next to the sink, and turned around, heaving an exasperated sigh. "Nothing," I said. "I've found nothing."

I might have told her about the computer if I had thought that the information would get her off my back, even for a moment, but I had a feeling it would have the exact opposite effect. I had a feeling it would only make her turn the screws tighter. And they were plenty tight already, thank you.

"You can't be serious," she said as I brushed by her into the room. "You really expect me to believe that after a week and a half you've found nothing?"

"You can believe whatever you want to believe," I told her, sitting blithely on my bed. "This country was founded on that principle."

Natasha clucked her tongue and rolled her eyes. She pressed the heels of her hands into her forehead like I was giving her a migraine. Good. She deserved mind-splitting pain. That'd teach her to blackmail me.

"What's the problem here, Reed?" she asked me. "Was I not explicit enough when I told you exactly what I would do if you didn't help me?"

"No. You were plenty explicit, thanks. *Star* magazine explicit," I told her. "The problem is that if they are hiding anything, they're hiding it very well. This is Noelle we're dealing with here, remember? You really think she's going to leave incriminating evidence out on her bulletin board?"

Natasha unclenched a bit at this. Not even she could argue with that logic.

"Just . . . be patient," I said, wondering how long, exactly, it would take a person with zero computer experience to crack someone else's password. I picked up my copy of *Beowulf*, which we were reading for English class—at least, everyone else was, while I had yet to have time to crack it—and leaned back on my denim husband. "I'm doing everything I can."

I settled in and opened to page one.

"Well, do it faster," Natasha said.

Then she flicked off the light before I could get past the first word.

the password is . . .

After two full mornings of typing in everything I knew about Ariana into her password screen and getting nowhere, I was at a complete loss. I needed help. I needed someplace to start. I needed to pick someone else's brain and get some ideas.

But how was I supposed to do that without anyone knowing *why* I was doing it?

This was the question bouncing around in my brain as I walked into the library one rainy afternoon. I had a plan, but I had very little confidence that it would work. Unfortunately, it was all I had. I knew that the junior class had a huge history exam coming up and half of Billings and Ketlar would be there studying. I made a beeline for the very back of the stacks, where I knew the girls from my dorm normally set up camp.

Bingo. At one table I had found Kiran, Taylor, Rose, London, Vienna, Josh, and Gage. They were all bent over their books, some taking notes, others whispering to each other in low tones. There was a single empty chair at the end of the table.

I took a deep breath. Here went nothing.

I walked over and sat down with a frustrated huff, placing my books on the table. Everyone looked up, happy for a distraction.

"What's the matter, Reed?" Taylor asked.

"Nothing. It's just this current events paper for modern civ," I said. "I have to write eight pages on that whole hacking scandal."

Kiran and Taylor exchanged a look. They weren't buying it. There was no way they were buying it. And why would they? It was a complete fabrication.

"You mean that thing at that high school in New York?" Josh said.

"I heard about that!" London put in, excited. "Someone hacked into all the students' computers and posted a list of all the illicit Web sites they were looking at. So scandalous."

"Those poor bastards had all their porn deleted," Gage said. "That's not scandal. It's a crying shame."

"Well, there are about a million articles on it and it's ridiculous trying to sift through it all," I said, lifting out a Xeroxed page. "Plus it's scary. Did you guys know that ninety percent of high school students use something obvious for their password? Like a boyfriend's name or a birthday?"

Everyone just stared at me. Was I the worst actress ever, or what?

"I would never use something that lame," Gage said.

"Yeah. You just spell curse words backward," Josh said with a laugh.

"Dude!" Gage complained, whacking him with the back of his hand.

"I would never use anything that obvious," Rose said, turning the page in her history book. "I just use random characters."

So not what I wanted to hear. If Ariana was using random characters, I was screwed.

"How do you remember them?" Vienna asked.

"I just force myself," Rose said. "I repeat it over and over until it's in there. Four, dash, dollar sign, eight, *J*, star. Four, dash, dollar sign, eight, *J*, star."

"Nice one! Now we all know your password!" Gage said.

Rose turned beet red. "Well, that's not my password *now*."

"Yes, it is! Yes, it is!" London trilled, bouncing up and down in her chair, her long earrings slapping her in the face. "We know your password! We know your password!"

"Oh, yeah? Repeat it back to me," Rose said flatly.

London cleared her throat and looked at the ceiling. "Four, dash, dollop of . . . A . . . J . . ." Everyone laughed and London lost steam, slumping. "Crap."

"It's okay," Vienna said, patting her back. "It's not like Rose has anything good on her computer."

Rose shot Vienna a *bite me* look and got back to studying.

"Personally, I always use song titles," Kiran said, lifting a shoulder. "I think a lot of people do that. Like book titles or movie titles or poems . . . CDs—"

Titles. That sounded like something Ariana might do. I made a surreptitious note in the margin of the Xeroxed article.

"You know, Reed, I read somewhere that some huge percentage of people actually write down their password and keep it somewhere close to their computer," Taylor said. "They jot it down on a special day in the calendar or something. You know, just in case they ever forget it."

"Really?" I said, intrigued.

"Yeah. I bet I could find the article if you want me to," Taylor said. "I save *everything.*"

Like I didn't know that already. Of course, she had no way of knowing how much time I had already spent under her bed.

"Don't worry about the paper too much," Kiran said, returning to her own work. "Mr. Kline has a very lax grading system."

"There's a theory going around that he only reads the first page of everything anyway," Josh said.

"That's good news," I said, feigning relief.

Everyone returned to their books and I realized that the conversation was closed. There was no way to open it again without looking completely obvious. But at least they had given me a few places to start. Now all I had to do was put these new theories to the test.

transparencies

I should have been studying for my French quiz. I should have been taking notes for my history test. I should have been reading *Beowulf*. I should have been asking Kiran if I could raid her closet for an outfit to wear out to dinner with Whit. I should have been doing any one of these things. Instead I was at Natasha's desk with the Easton Academy website open on her computer, bent over a notebook, brainstorming potential passwords for Ariana's computer.

Taking a cue from Kiran, I had started scouring old issues of the Easton literary magazine, the *Quill*, online. If Ariana's password *was* in fact a title, then I figured it might be the title of one of her very own poems. Unfortunately she had published at least three and sometimes as many as seven poems in each and every issue of the *Quill*, going back to her freshman year. My list of poem titles already filled an entire page.

I sighed and closed the window containing last year's final *Quill* issue and double clicked on the latest one—published only last month. I knew that Ariana had at least five poems tucked inside its pages. I opened the table-of-contents page and jotted down the titles:

"Transparency"

"Endless Fall"

"The Other"

"Scarecrow"

"The Dark Age"

Ariana was a very lighthearted, carefree girl.

Suddenly the door to my room opened, sending my heart into unhealthy spasms. It only got worse when Ariana walked in, followed closely by Noelle and Taylor. I slapped my notebook closed and reached for the laptop's screen, but realized it would look far too suspicious. Besides, they were already behind me. Noelle placed a paper bag on the floor near the wall. I had a feeling I didn't want to know what was in it.

"Using Natasha's computer, huh?" Noelle said, leaning both hands on the back of the chair so that I tipped slightly backward. "Hope you asked or she might turn you in to the Gestapo."

"Looking at the *Quill*, are we?" Ariana said, hovering behind me. "Getting ideas?" she asked, her eyes dancing.

My heart completely stopped. For a second my life flashed before my eyes. She knew what I was doing. She was actually psychic.

"Ideas? For what?" I choked out.

Ariana smiled slowly. "Well, your writing, of course. I know you're a big reader. I always wondered if you might be a writer as well."

"Oh! Right!" I said, all the blood in my body rushing to my face. Of course she didn't know what I was doing. How could she possibly? "I *am* a writer. I'm actually thinking about joining. You know, the *Quill*."

If it hadn't been for self-preservation purposes, I might have been alarmed that I was getting so good at lying.

"That's great. We'd love to have you," Ariana said with a small smile. She looked at Noelle, who was, for some reason, grinning as well. "What do you write?"

Now I reached over and clicked the laptop closed, mostly to stall for time. I hadn't written anything creatively since first grade, when I'd written a short story titled "Animal Crackers" that had been universally panned by all the six-year-olds in my class.

"Uh . . . essays, mostly," I said. "But lately I haven't really had much time."

Thanks to you guys, my tone implied. *You and your chore list are so the reason my muse has gone missing.*

"And you're about to have even less," Noelle said happily.

Everything inside of me slumped. "Why?"

"It's the windows," Taylor said, her expression bordering on apologetic. "They're a disgrace."

The windows? Didn't Easton employ a maintenance staff for this kind of thing? "What windows?" I asked, even though I already knew the answer.

"All of them," Noelle said, taking my notebook out of my hands. I snatched at it, but she tossed it on my bed. She reached into the paper bag and produced a bottle of Windex and a stack of fresh rags. "And you can start with mine."

weak stomach

"It's going to rain," Ariana said, turning her blue eyes toward the roiling sky the following evening. "We should hurry."

I wrapped my scarf around my neck and scurried down the library stairs after her. The last hour had been spent listening to Ariana and her fellow *Quill* editors discuss the merits and flaws of various submissions for the latest issue. Since, in my moment of panic, I had expressed an interest, Ariana had invited me to come along and see what it was like. Now, having listened to these pretentious people tearing apart one another's work, I could sum it up in three words:

Not for me.

Still, I was touched that she had asked me. It meant that she thought I was worthy of sharing one of her favorite things. If only she knew that whenever I had started scribbling in my notebook during the meeting I hadn't been taking notes on the poems but jotting down new ideas for her password.

That morning, while I was supposed to be scrubbing floors, I had searched Ariana's room for a calendar or a date book, hoping to put Taylor's theory to the test, but had found nothing. If Ariana had a planner, she kept it with her at all times. After that failure, I had spent half an hour rapidly typing in every potential keyword I could come up with, flinching at every creak of the floor and every chirp of a bird outside the window. None of them had worked. Now I was on a mission. I had spent too much of my time on this already. I had to crack that password, if only to be able to tell myself that I had succeeded.

So I had spent most of my classes brainstorming more and more potential passwords and writing them down in my trusty notebook. At this rate I was going to flunk out of school, but at least I would know whether or not the Billings Girls had gotten Leanne Shore thrown out. Yeah. It would all be worth it.

Ha.

"So, what did you think?" Ariana asked me as we speed-walked along the cobbled paths. "Did you enjoy it?"

"It was interesting," I said in a noncommittal tone. "I don't know if I feel comfortable tearing apart people's poems, though."

"Why?" Ariana asked.

"Well, those are their most personal thoughts and feelings. It has to take a lot to put that out there," I said. "And you guys just sat there throwing out words like *pathetic* and *pedestrian* and *cliché*. That one girl was on the staff and you said she had no original thought. Right in front of her."

"I know. It's not easy," Ariana said, shaking her head. She

hugged her notebooks to her chest and curled her slim shoulders in against the wind, her chin tucked down so it was almost hidden behind the books. "But if you're going to put something on a page and ask people to read it, you have to be able to handle the criticism."

"I guess," I said as we reached the front door to Billings. "It just seemed mean."

Ariana stopped and stared at the door. The sky chose that moment to open up. A fat raindrop plopped right in the middle of my forehead.

"Look, Reed, if you can't handle it then maybe you shouldn't come back," Ariana said rather harshly. She placed her hand on the door handle and gripped hard enough for her knuckles to turn white.

"I never said I couldn't *handle* it," I told her. "I just—"

"No. You don't have the stomach for it," she said, looking me in the eye. "And that's fine, but just don't pretend to be something you're not. It's a waste of your time. And mine."

Whoa. Okay. Where had *that* come from?

Ariana whipped open the door to Billings and strode inside. For a long moment I stood there, feeling as if I'd just been slapped. Who the hell did she think she was, talking to me that way? She didn't know me well enough to know what I was or was not capable of.

Anger seared my skin as I walked into Billings after her. I couldn't just let this one go without saying anything. First the implication that I had something to do with Thomas's disappearance and now this? What, exactly, was Ariana's problem with me? As I entered the foyer, I expected her to be on her way upstairs, but the place was deserted. Then I noticed that all the lights in the common room off the entryway had been dimmed. I slowly pulled off my scarf and shook it out as I went over to inspect the situation. The half-dozen couches and chairs had been pulled together to face the big-screen TV, and there were all my dorm mates, gathered together with snacks and drinks, watching the latest Orlando Bloom movie.

It was a very cozy scene and, after all the stress of the past few days, looked like the perfect antidote to my two tons of stress.

"Hi, Reed," Taylor whispered from her spot on the first couch. Kiran glanced over her shoulder and fluttered a wave. Rose looked up and smiled.

"Hey," I replied, already scoping out a spot.

Across the room near the fireplace, Ariana was just settling in on an overstuffed pillow at Noelle's feet. Noelle pulled a throw off the back of her chair and passed it to Ariana, never taking her eyes from the screen. She lifted an hors d'oeuvre—some kind of cracker, cheese, and black gunk combination—from a platter on the table next to her and placed the entire thing in her mouth.

"What's all this?" I asked.

"Movie night," Rose whispered. "We do it once a month."

"Sweet," I said.

"Not for you, glass-licker," Noelle said in full voice. "You need to get back to the windows."

I blinked. "But I finished the windows."

"Yeah. And they have more streaks than my mom's last dye job," Cheyenne said.

"Go to it," Noelle said. "Maybe you'll be able to catch the last five minutes. But I doubt it."

Everyone laughed. All fifteen of them. Fifteen times the humiliation. Ariana looked at me with those eerie eyes and smirked.

"Would you bring my bag upstairs for me, Reed?" she asked, holding out her messenger bag. "Thanks," she added sweetly.

Then I saw Natasha was watching me, too, with a meaningful stare. I gave her a nod, feeling very *CSI*. There couldn't have been a more perfect opportunity to get back to my project. Back to that computer. And little did Ariana know she had just handed me the one thing I might need to finally break her password wide open. Her bag. Which undoubtedly had her planner inside.

Ariana thought I had no stomach? Just watch me.

success

An hour later my eyes were dry, my neck was tight, and a headache throbbed at the back of my skull. I checked my watch every two-and-a-half minutes, wondering exactly how long it was going to take Orlando to find love. Did I have fifteen minutes or another hour?

"Okay, come on, Reed," I said through my teeth, shaking out my hands.

I flipped to the next page in Ariana's planner and turned it over on the floor at my side. Taylor's theory had turned out to be both a boon and a curse. At first I had thought I would just check Ariana's birthday and see if she had anything written there. That was before I realized that I had no idea when Ariana's birthday was. So instead I had started to flip through page by page, figuring the special days would be obvious, that she'd have written *Dad's birthday* on a certain date, or *Parents' anniversary* somewhere in there.

I was wrong. Nothing was obvious in Ariana's planner, other

than the fact that she was a doodler. A doodler and a jotter who brainstormed poems and titles in every available space on every available page. Yes, there were poem titles on some dates, but there was no way of knowing if the dates held any significance. So I had spent the last hour typing in pretty much every word I found in any given date square.

Pretty soon, my knuckles were going to seize up. Early onset arthritis. That was where this mission was going to get me.

I took a deep breath. I just had to keep at it for a few more minutes. Then I would call it a night and at least wipe down Noelle and Ariana's windows—which looked streak-free to me—so that they would think I had followed orders.

I was on April. April fifth had a single word in its square. I took a deep breath and started to type.

Rubber band. *R-U-B-B-E-R-B-A-N-D*. Enter.

Invalid password! the screen replied.

Okay . . . next. Slammed. *S-L-A-M-M-E-D*. Enter.

Invalid password!

I groaned. I scanned the calendar, looking for something even remotely intriguing, and my eyes fell on the last day of April. April 30. In big, red letters was the word *home*. Then, underneath that, in much smaller letters, the title of one of her more recent poems: "The Other." That one had been published in last month's *Quill*.

I took a deep breath. My fingers were trembling. Okay. "The Other." Two words.

T-H-E [space] *O-T-H-E-R*. Enter.

Invalid password!

Somewhere nearby a door slammed. My heart was in my mouth. I closed the computer and was about to stash it away, but instead I froze. I froze and listened. Footsteps. Footsteps coming closer . . .

Oh, God, no. I scrambled to put everything back. I almost dropped the computer. I was never going to get it all in there in time. . . .

And then the footsteps passed by the door. They were going back downstairs. I sat down hard on my butt and breathed. Everything was shaking. I should just bag this. Just bag it and start over tomorrow. But when was I ever going to get an opportunity like this again?

Slowly, I opened the computer again. I would just try this last one and that would be it.

Okay. Theother. One word.

T-H-E-O-T-H-E-R. Enter.

There was a beep. My pulse raced. The drive whirred to life, the screen went black, then came up with a blue sky background and the two sweetest words I had ever seen on a computer screen.

Welcome, Ariana!

Holy crap. I was in! Holy mother of—I had done it! I wanted to jump up off the floor and scream and yell and improvise a dance of joy. But that wouldn't have been the best idea, what with the old creaky floors and the fifteen girls watching Orlando in rapt silence under my feet.

Deep breath, Reed. I scrounged in my bag and found the

floppy disk I had brought along just in case there was anything worth copying. I shoved it in the slot on the side of the computer and tried to calm my heart. If it kept pounding that loud, it would drown out any noises from downstairs, and I couldn't get caught. Especially not now.

There were several file icons on Ariana's desktop, each marked with a year. I clicked open the most recent and there were nothing but Word files inside. Poems. Hundreds of poems. Some with titles I recognized from the *Quill*, most with ones I did not. But was one of these an incriminating file in disguise? Was one of these "poems" actually some kind of anti-Leanne rant that might prove Ariana wanted to hurt her in some way? Who knew? My heart filled with sick, frustrated desperation. I did not have time to click open and read a hundred or more poems.

I scrolled down in the window, looking for who knew what. At the very bottom was one single file icon. A file within the file. It was marked "projects."

Okay. This could be something. I double clicked. Inside were several more Word documents, each with initials as their titles. EP, CS, IP, NL, TL, IM, and then LS.

LS. Leanne Shore.

My entire mind went blank. This was it. A file on Leanne. I suppose that part of me had always thought it was impossible. That Noelle and Ariana could never have gotten someone kicked out of school for no good reason. But here it was. I was about to have the proof.

Reluctantly salivating, I opened the file. A Word document

popped up and filled the screen. At the top, the words *Latin Studies*. Then, *Notes from 8/5*. My whole body slumped and I almost laughed. Apparently, Ariana had spent her summer taking classes. In Latin. Studies.

Nothing to do with Leanne. Ariana was innocent.

I took a breath and closed the document. I listened for footsteps and heard nothing. Apparently Orlando was still doing his thing. I decided to check out the other initialed documents, just to satisfy my curiosity, so that I wouldn't have gone through all this for nothing. I opened EP. It was a list of women's names with "yes" or "no" next to each one and a total at the bottom, some kind of RSVP list. Maybe Ariana had helped her mom throw a party or something. Next up was CS. I opened it and my heart took a nosedive.

As I Lay Dying, Faulkner, 1930.

Their Eyes Were Watching God, Hurston, 1937.

Invisible Man, Ellison, 1947.

It was a crib sheet. A list in a tiny font set on 3 x 5 paper. And from the looks of the information, it was a senior English crib sheet. Exactly the class Leanne Shore had cheated in. And what had the administration used as their damning evidence?

Crib sheets.

If these matched the crib sheets that had sealed Leanne's fate, then it was all true. Natasha was right. Noelle and her friends *had* framed Leanne. They had gotten her kicked out of school. But why? Just because she was a suck-up and she annoyed Noelle? Was that really a reason to mess with someone's life?

Dying to know more now, I opened the file marked IM. Sure

enough, a file full of copied IM messages filled the screen. They were mostly between Ariana and Noelle. My eyes scanned the first messages. They all seemed mundane. Conversations about homework and parties—nothing out of the ordinary.

Then I saw my name and all the air rushed out of me. I stopped to read.

> ***Ariana***: so we're definitely doing this
> **Noelle_1**: DEFINITELY. We decided we wanted Reed right?
> ***Ariana***: yes. and lattimer is on board. kiran got her a free pass at manolo 4 her silence.
> **Noelle_1**: PERFECT! Lattimer is 2 easy. So we're ready to do it? You have the cribs?
> ***Ariana***: all set. just tell me when and where.
> **Noelle_1**: TOMORROW. We'll get Reed in here by the weekend. And L out. Thank God!
> ***Ariana***: you are so bad!
> **Noelle_1**: And it feels SO GOOD . . .

I could not breathe. Couldn't move. Couldn't have even saved myself if the entire dorm had walked in at that very moment.

They had done it for me, to create a place for me in Billings. This had all happened because of me.

I heard a creak on the stairs and suddenly came to life. I didn't have time to think about this. Quickly I copied all the initialed files onto my disk, just in case there happened to be something more worth reading. I shoved the disk into the back pocket of my jeans, then shut the computer down and replaced everything as I'd found it. I was just closing the trunk when I heard voices downstairs. The party was breaking up. I shoved the trunk into the back of the closet, closed the doors, grabbed my stuff, and fled.

I knew everyone would be coming up the front, so I raced for the safety of the back stairwell. Once inside, I slumped down on the steps and struggled to catch my breath.

They had framed Leanne because of me. It was my fault Leanne had been booted. My fault Natasha was so upset she was willing to blackmail people and sneak around behind their backs. It was all for me. So that I could live here. So that I could be a Billings Girl.

It was sick. It was twisted. It was evil. But it was also for me. No one had ever done anything like this for me before. They had risked their own futures to get me into Billings and solidify mine. As disgusted as I was, I was also more than a little bit flattered.

And how had I repaid them? I had snooped through their rooms. Uncovered their most embarrassing secrets. For a moment I was overcome with shame. These were my friends, and I had betrayed them.

But I still had one question. *Why* were they my friends? Why had they brought me to Billings at all? What were they getting out of it? Why did they even want me here? Just so they could order me around? It didn't make any sense. None of this made any sense.

A door slammed right above me and I was on my feet again, racing down the stairs fast enough to keep up with my pulse. I had to get back to my room anyway. Get back there and think. I had the evidence now. I had what Natasha needed. The question was, would I ever share it with her?

suspicious eyes

The next morning while Natasha was in the shower, I threw on jeans and a sweatshirt, tossed my hair into a ponytail, and snuck out, closing the door as quietly as humanly possible. I had risen early and had already redone all the first-floor windows in an effort to avoid being in the room when her alarm went off. Now was the perfect chance to bail before she could ask me if I'd found anything and before the other girls could strong-arm me into more chores.

It was a cool, cloudy morning and I shrugged into my coat as I quickly dialed Thomas's room on my cell phone. I hurried away from Billings, hoisting my bag over my shoulder as I held the phone to my ear. The campus was as silent as a graveyard. My breath made steam clouds in the cold morning air. The marigolds that lined the walk to Billings were bent from the weight of the frost that covered their petals. I struggled to button my coat with one frigid hand. Josh picked up on the fifth ring.

"'Lo?" he asked. He was still asleep.

"Josh, I'm so sorry to wake you."

"Who is this?" he asked.

"It's Reed," I said. Suddenly I felt as if someone was watching me. I paused at the intersection of the path to the girls' dorms and the path to the library and looked around. The quad was completely deserted except for a squirrel zipping here and there under one of the benches.

"Reed. What's wrong?" he asked me. "Is it Thomas? Did you hear from him?"

"No," I said, squirming at the mention of the name. "I just have to talk to you about something. Can you meet me in the caf in, like, fifteen minutes?"

"Uh . . . sure," he said. "I'll be right there."

"Thanks," I told him.

The moment I hung up the phone, I felt a chill down my back. I whipped around and my heart rocketed into my throat. I gasped, startled, and then choked. Detective Hauer was three feet behind me. His brow creased as he approached me, his black trench coat billowing behind him.

"Are you all right, Miss Brennan?" he asked me.

I pounded on my chest with my free hand and tried to get control of my cough. *Miss Brennan*. He'd remembered my name. He'd met about five hundred kids over the past two weeks and he'd remembered my name. That could not be good.

"I'm fine," I said. "Fine. You just scared me."

"Sorry," he replied, though he didn't look it. "I like a stroll in the morning. Clears my head."

He looked like he was waiting for a response, so I gave him one. "That's . . . nice."

"And you?" he said.

"And me what?"

"What are you doing out here so early?" he asked. "It was a long time ago, I admit, but I sort of remember liking my sleep as a teenager."

"Yeah, well, I'm an individual," I said with a laugh, throwing my hands out. I was acting like a derranged scarecrow.

"Who were you talking to?" he asked, eyeing my phone. He rubbed his hands together and blew into them.

"Oh, uh . . ." There didn't seem to be any reason to lie. "Josh. Josh Hollis. He's meeting me at breakfast."

"Thomas Pearson's roommate?" he said, raising his bushy eyebrows. "That Josh Hollis?"

Why did he have to make it sound suspicious? What the heck was wrong with me meeting Josh?

I shrugged. "He's the only one I know." Then I made an elaborate show of checking my watch. "Ooh. I gotta go. I'm gonna be late," I said, backing up. "Enjoy your walk."

He nodded, narrowing his eyes slightly. "Enjoy your break-fast."

"I will! Thanks!" I replied, trying my hardest to seem unaffected.

It didn't work. I could feel him watching me all the way across the quad and it was all I could do to keep myself from turning around and checking to see if I was right. But when I finally reached the cafeteria, sweating from exertion and nerves, I couldn't take it anymore. I paused and pretended to search through my bag for something. As I did so, I glanced out the corner of my eye. There was Detective Hauer, standing alone in the center of campus.

Watching me.

idealism

For the first time in days I was able to go through the breakfast line and get what *I* wanted and *only* what I wanted. I knew that as soon as the Billings Girls arrived I would be back up here, filling their orders, but for now I was going to enjoy the freedom. I deserved it after everything I'd been through this morning.

Two pieces of bacon, one slice of peanut butter toast, and a bowl full of Apple Jacks later, I emerged from the line and walked over to our usual table. I started with the toast, hoping to calm my uneasy stomach before moving on to the sugar and the grease. The cavernous cafeteria was so undisturbed, I could see the individual dust particles dancing in the shafts of sun coming through the skylights. I watched Josh enter through the front door, stick to the wall on his way to the line, and emerge moments later with coffee and three doughnuts.

"So, I'm intrigued," he said, sitting down in front of me. He chomped into a cinnamon doughnut, spraying the brown powder everywhere. His curls were mashed on one side and stuck straight up on the other, reminding me that just a few minutes ago he had been curled up in his bed, warm and cozy, and that he'd hoisted himself out of his slumber for me.

"Okay, hypothetically . . ."

Josh dropped the doughnut. "I love a good 'hypothetically,'" he said, leaning his elbows on the table.

I laughed. "Hypothetically," I repeated for his benefit, "if you found out that one of the guys in your dorm had broken the honor code . . . would you tell?"

Josh raised his eyebrows, then looked down at his plate and blew out a breath.

"I mean, I know you're *supposed* to tell, but, in reality . . . would you?" I asked.

Josh nodded once and lifted his head. "Definitely."

"Really?"

The double doors opened and a clump of students filed in. We wouldn't be alone for long.

"Yes. No question," Josh said, sipping his coffee. "You signed a contract. We all did. I know it's probably not cool or whatever to say this, but that actually means something to me. When you commit to something, you don't go back on your word. Besides, it's the right thing to do. If someone does something wrong, they should be called on it. Case closed."

Damn. Boy took his hypothetical very seriously. For some reason, his conviction made me squirm. I dropped the toast and pushed my tray away.

"Tell me how you really feel," I joked, trying to lighten my own mood.

"How he really feels is idiotic."

Startled, we both looked up to find Whittaker hovering at the end of the table. Where had he come from?

"No offense intended," he said to Josh.

"Uh . . . none taken," Josh said facetiously. He jumped his chair forward until the table constricted his chest so that Whittaker could get by. Whit pulled out the chair next to Josh and settled in. He took a long sip of his grapefruit juice and smacked his lips.

"I didn't intend to eavesdrop, but I couldn't help overhearing," Whittaker began, resting his wrists on the edge of the table like a well-mannered boy. "Reed, if there is, in fact, someone in Billings who has cheated . . . you cannot, under any circumstances, turn them in."

"What?" Josh blurted.

"Your opinion is kind of naïve, don't you think?" Whittaker said, picking up his fork and toying with the eggs on his plate. "Not to mention hypocritical."

Josh pushed back a bit and crossed his arms over his chest. "Wow. Called a naïve hypocrite before I even get to morning services. That's a first."

"Well, it's true," Whittaker said. "You sit there talking about how people in the wrong should be called on their actions, but did you ever do anything about the fact that your roommate was a drug dealer?"

I felt as if the entire room had just been hit by a cold north wind. Goose bumps everywhere. Josh's face went ashen.

"That's none of your business," he said.

"It is when you're filling my friend's head with empty morality," Whittaker told him.

Then, satisfied that he'd rendered Josh speechless, Whittaker turned and looked me dead in the eye.

"You do not want to ostracize yourself from the women of Billings, Reed," he said. "Trust me. Not if you want to have a life after you graduate this place. *That's* reality."

I swallowed hard and looked at Josh. He rolled his eyes, but said nothing. I realized that Whittaker had just hit upon the very reason Josh's idealism had made me squirm. Ever since my first day at Easton, all I had heard was that the Billings Girls had the brightest futures of anyone at this school. It was all about connections. The connections got you everywhere. If I turned in Noelle and the others, would all my Billings connections be severed for life? Would everything I had gained by getting in there be automatically obliterated?

"You know I'm right," Whittaker said haughtily. "I can see it in your eyes."

"Excuse me," Josh said, shoving away from the table. "I'm feeling a little nauseous all of a sudden."

He grabbed one of the remaining doughnuts and stormed out. Whittaker took a deep breath and shook his head. "He'll learn," he said. "Eventually."

I watched Whittaker shovel eggs into his mouth and was suddenly disgusted by the very sight of him. Even if he was right on some level, something about his all-knowing tone completely turned me off. Who had died and made him the fourth wise man?

"Now that we're alone . . ," he said, lifting himself out of his chair and taking Josh's, so that he was sitting directly across from me. "I wanted to let you know that all the arrangements are in place for Friday night. I'll pick you up on the circle at six o'clock. That should give us plenty of time to get to Boston for our reservation. I am so looking forward to this, Reed."

The way he was looking at me made me feel almost feverish with revulsion. There was desire in his eyes, plain and simple and obvious. He thought that this date was going to end the same way that night in the woods had.

Well, he was probably hoping to avoid the vomit.

"Are you excited?" he asked.

It's for Thomas. It's so that you can go to the Legacy and see Thomas.

"Sure," I said weakly.

Then he reached out and took my hand. He covered it with both his big, clumsy, oafish ones. Staring at them, I had sudden flashes of another pair of hands. Thin but strong. Self-assured and tender. Hands that had caused me to flush with pleasure every time they touched me.

I glanced to the left and saw several junior girls from one of the other dorms eyeing me with envy. Everyone knew what

Whittaker's gesture meant. It meant I was one step closer to being his plus-one. And they were one step closer to sitting at home on Halloween night.

"Maybe after dinner we can stop somewhere," Whittaker said, coloring slightly. "Somewhere we can be alone."

His thumb pressed into my palm. My stomach turned and I pulled my hand away. There was no way I could do this. No way I could sit in a car with this guy for hours each way wondering when he was going to make his move, dreading the thought of his lips on mine. He was a sweet guy—an awkward, hopeful, sweet guy who was just trying. I could see that. But he was trying on the wrong girl.

"Is something wrong?" he asked, his eyes wide.

"No. I'm fine," I said, standing. "I just remembered that I left my history text in my room and I . . . I need that for class. I better go."

"Okay, then. I'll . . . see you later?" he asked, lifting himself out of his chair, ever the gentleman.

"Sure. Yes. Definitely," I said.

But even as I shoved my way out into the sunshine, I was formulating a plan. There had to be a way for me to get to the Legacy without Whittaker. There just had to be.

pre-party

That evening I paused outside Noelle and Ariana's room. I had just heard voices coming from inside and had automatically stopped to listen. It was a reflex. Now that I knew the extent of their secrets, part of me was dying to uncover more. But I couldn't make out anything other than murmurs and laughter, and then I remembered I was here to ask a favor. Eavesdropping was probably not the best way to endear myself. I straightened up, steeled myself, and knocked.

"Entrez!" Noelle announced.

Inside the lights were dim and candles flickered on every available surface, filling the air with their musky scents. Noelle, Ariana, Kiran, and Taylor were all gathered in a circle in their pajamas and robes. Taylor sat in one of the desk chairs, pulled close to Ariana's bed, while the others were seated on the mattress. Ariana held up a wineglass and Kiran tipped a bottle over it, filling it with deep red liquid.

"Reed! So good to see you!" Noelle trilled. "Come! Have wine! We're playing I Never."

I Never. These girls had nothing better to do than play I Never?
On a weeknight? Shouldn't they be reading or writing papers or
perhaps plotting to have someone else booted out of school?
Behind me, in Ariana's closet, I could feel the presence of the
trunk and the computer as if they had been dipped in radioactive
waste and were now throbbing brightly like a beacon, mocking
me. Reminding me of what I had done. What I knew.

"*I* never . . . got drunk and bribed my father's pilot to fly me to
Rome so I could have real pasta!" Taylor announced.

"Oh!" Noelle cheered.

Kiran clucked her tongue. "No fair getting so specific!" she
said, then downed half her wine.

Her father had a *pilot*. Her father had a pilot who would fly to
Rome on a moment's notice.

"Come on, Reed! What have *you* never done?" Noelle asked
mirthfully.

"Actually, I wanted to talk to you guys about something," I said.

"Not until you give us an 'I never,'" Ariana said, her eyes
gleaming.

Great. Nothing like being put on the spot. I racked my brain
for something, anything, that wouldn't make me sound totally
lame.

"I never . . . had sex in a car," I said finally.

Noelle spit out a laugh and drank the rest of her wine, as did
Kiran and Taylor, laughing the whole way. Ariana, however, just
smiled.

"Really, Ariana?" Kiran asked, nonplussed. "Not even a limo? They can be *very* comfortable."

"I'm gonna start calling you Prude," Noelle put in.

Ariana simply sighed, as if this was all just too pedestrian, and set her glass aside. "What's going on, Reed?"

"Nothing. It's just . . . it's about the Legacy."

A mutual look was exchanged between the four of them. "Pull up a chair," Kiran said, lifting the wine bottle.

I crossed over to Noelle's desk chair, cleared about ten cashmere, silk, and angora sweaters onto her bed, and carried the chair over. As I settled in, I had their full attention. This was odd.

"What's the problem?" Noelle asked, crossing her legs at the knee and leaning forward like a concerned talk-show hostess. Except no talk-show hostess I had ever seen ever waved a glass of wine around in front of her live studio audience. "Has Whittaker not asked you yet?"

"No. He hasn't. But it's not that," I said. "I mean, I'm sure he will—"

"Wow. Look at the ego on this one," Kiran said, taking a sip of her wine. I chose to ignore the comment.

"It's just . . . I don't exactly want to go with him," I said. "Can't any of you get me in? I could be *your* plus-one," I said, looking at Noelle.

Instantly, she scoffed. She sat up straight and swung her thick, dark hair over her shoulder. "You're not getting it, Reed. *We* can't even all get in without help."

I had no response to that except to stare incredulously. The Billings Girls couldn't get in without help? How was that even possible? I had a hard time imagining them being shut out of anything.

"Come on," I said finally.

Noelle and Ariana laughed. Kiran picked at a cuticle, her cheeks flushing, while Taylor simply stared into her wineglass.

"Did you not hear me the other day? This party is exclusive. I'm the only person in all of Billings who even *gets* a plus-one."

"Well, you and Cheyenne," Taylor said.

"Right. Cheyenne. The D.A.R. herself," Noelle said. "Why do I always forget about Cheyenne?"

The other girls chuckled as if they all knew exactly why Cheyenne was so forgettable. Another joke I hadn't been let it on. But I had to focus on the aneurysm at hand.

"You're kidding," I said. "You guys can't bring dates?"

"Well, I can," Noelle said, leaning back. "But I'm taking Dash."

"Dash can't get in?" I asked. He who'd read me the rules of the night? He who'd acted all superior about the whole thing?

"Please," Noelle said. "He's only second generation. His grandfather went to, like, P.S. 121 in the Bronx or something."

"But then he made his first million by the time he was twenty-two," Kiran added. "Real estate."

"It's a real come-from-nothing story. You should ask him to tell you sometime," Noelle said sardonically.

"Who's Cheyenne taking?" I asked, even though I knew there was no way in hell she'd take pity on me.

"Her little Boston boyfriend," Kiran answered. "What's his name? Dork? Doofball?"

"Dougray," Ariana answered, putting on an imperious English accent.

"Well, do we know anyone else who gets a plus-one?" I asked hopefully.

"Just Gage. And he's taking Kiran," Ariana said.

"Yeah. I gotta be Gage Coolidge's date. *So* looking forward to it," Kiran said.

"That's what you get for being a frosh," Noelle said, sipping her drink. Then, off my confused look, she placed her hand next to her mouth and loud-whispered, "First generation. Oh! But then, I guess you are, too," she added sweetly.

"Sorry, Reed. But there's nothing we can do," Ariana told me.

"That's why we were trying to set you up with Whit," Noelle said. "He's basically your only shot."

"Wait a minute, Kiran. *You* can't even get in? You're a supermodel," I pointed out.

Kiran's head bobbed as she laughed once, derisively. "Sweetie, Scarlett Johansson couldn't get into this thing unless Whittaker brought her." She drained the rest of her cup and sucked her cheeks together slightly as she swallowed. The look she gave me was all meaning. Like, *You want to go to this party. Don't fuck it up.*

Noelle stood up and then bent at the waist so that her eyes were mere inches from mine. I tried to avert my gaze so I didn't have to stare straight into her eyes, but when I did I saw directly down her silk night shirt and almost melted from embarrassment. Eye contact it was.

"Reed, when are you going to figure out that we do everything for a reason?" she said, placing her hand on my shoulder. "We set you up with Whittaker so that you could go to the Legacy. We don't want to go without you."

Suddenly I felt all warm inside.

"We will, but we don't want to," Kiran added with a giggle.

Noelle stood straight again, then she moved over to the window. Staring out across the quad, she took a long drink from her glass and then looked at me.

"So, what's it gonna be?"

Noelle wanted me there. Thomas was going to be there. And at this point, I was also salivating to see what all this hype was about. And a party that even Kiran couldn't get into just by flashing a little leg had to be intense. Seriously.

I took a deep breath and turned to Kiran. "Can I borrow some clothes for Friday night? I have a date. With Whittaker."

my knight

Mrs. Lattimer walked me across the quad and over to the circle on Friday night, her heels clicking quickly even though we were moving at a snail's pace. Apparently while *on* campus I needed a chaperone, but they were going to let me go off campus with Whittaker alone. Maybe Mrs. Lattimer was supposed to make sure that I wasn't, in fact, boarding some party bus to Montreal. To make sure I didn't leave campus unless I did it with Whit.

The good news was I looked amazing in the outfit Kiran had lent me. Yes, even I was able to admit it. It was a sophisticated Calvin Klein black halter-style dress that hit just above the knee, with slim straps encircling my neck and accentuating my shoulders—which had been dusted with bronzer for a "sexy glow." It was topped by a gold brocade jacket—vintage Chanel—and the diamond earrings Whittaker had bought me. Kiran had insisted I wear my hair up, and when I'd revealed I knew how to do nothing other than a ponytail and a basic braid, she had grumbled but worked on me for an hour, gathering my brown locks up into a sophisticated loose-and-sexy bun. One pair of strappy, black Manolo Blahniks and the look was complete. The result? I was runway-worthy.

Too bad I felt more like I was walking down a plank.

"This is a very special privilege you've been granted tonight, Miss Brennan. I hope you realize that," Mrs. Lattimer said as we walked around Bradwell, which fronted the circle. She held the collar of her coat up to her chin to combat the chill. "Mrs. Whittaker doesn't do favors like this for just anyone."

I glanced at Mrs. Lattimer out of the corner of my eye. After what I had read about her on Ariana and Noelle's IM, I had a problem taking her seriously on any level. This woman had been bought off with a shopping spree. Bought off so that a bunch of overprivileged girls could get an innocent person thrown out of school. And I was supposed to, what? Look up to her?

"I know," I said flatly.

"I may have underestimated you when we first met," she said.

Fab. Now I could die happy.

"Uh, thanks. I guess."

"Walter must have some very strong feelings for you," she said, eyeing me shrewdly. Expectantly. Like I was going to share all the details of my sordid romance with her.

"I suppose," I said.

She narrowed her eyes at my blithe attitude and I had the distinct feeling that I had offended her. I guess meriting attention from the great Whittaker family was something I should have taken more seriously. I should have been flattered. All I wanted was to get this over with.

"Ah. There he is now. Your knight in shining armor," Mrs. Lattimer said as we came around the corner.

I don't know about the knight part, but there was definitely shining armor involved. Idling at the curb on the circle was a sleek silver sports car that was so slim and compact I had no idea how Whittaker might actually fit into it. The moment he saw us arrive, he stepped out from the driver's side and closed the door with a quiet pop. No clang, no bang, no shimmy. It was an expensive car's door slam, muffled by solid construction and what looked like a creamy leather interior.

"Good evening, Mrs. Lattimer," Whittaker said, walking over to us. He carried a huge bouquet of red roses and wore a black suit with a white shirt and a tie with tiny crests all over it. He actually looked quite handsome. Big and burly and handsome. The revulsion I had felt the other morning had, mercifully, passed—or at least put itself on hold in the face of more important things.

"Walter," Mrs. Lattimer said with a sober nod.

"Reed," he said. "You're stunning."

"Thanks," I replied lightly, trying to keep it casual.

He handed me the bouquet of roses, which smelled unbelievable. "These are for you."

"Thanks," I said again. Mrs. Lattimer cleared her throat— some sort of indication to me. "They're uh . . . lovely."

Whittaker smiled. "Shall we?"

He offered me his arm, as I had seen done in countless movies, and I almost laughed. Mrs. Lattimer nodded to me in a nudging way and I moved the bouquet to the crook of my left arm and slipped my right hand around his forearm. How I managed to do this without fidgeting or dropping anything, I have no idea. Apparently, watching all those movies had paid off.

Whittaker walked me over to the car and opened the door for me with a slight bow. I dropped into the bucket seat, tucking my jacket under my legs. When I looked out at Mrs. Lattimer again, she closed her eyes and shook her head.

Apparently there was a more graceful way to do that. At least Whittaker didn't seem to notice. He closed the door and turned to say a few words to Lattimer. I went to put the roses at my feet, but there was no room. They would have stuck up between my legs. I tried the backseat, but there was none. Finally I just laid them in my lap and buckled my seat belt beneath them.

I took a deep breath, inhaling the new-leather-and-roses scent, and sat back, attempting to keep this gray cloud that had been following me around all night at bay. Trying to keep from giving it a name. I ran my hand over the chrome dashboard and tried to be excited. This was amazing, really. This car, the dress, the flowers. Being whisked off campus to some swank restaurant while the rest of the school was back in the cafeteria eating Friday night pot roast. I was lucky. I really was.

My eyes filled with tears.

Too bad I was with the wrong guy.

The gray cloud enveloped me. Thomas was its name. This romantic evening should have been planned by him. I should have been with him. But instead he was out there who knew where, and I was here on a date with another guy.

The driver's-side door opened and Whittaker folded himself in behind the wheel. "I'm honored that you decided to come with me tonight, Reed," he said.

I took a deep breath and made myself smile. This was a means to an end. That was all it was. And if all went well here tonight, I'd be seeing Thomas soon enough.

"I'm honored you asked me."

birthday boy

On our approach to Boston I spotted the huge neon Citgo sign near the water and markers directing traffic to Fenway and Harvard. I stared out the windows at all the historic buildings, the domes and spires lit by the soft glow of strategically placed lights. On the water dozens of beautiful, pristine sailboats bobbed, tied up to docks, the water lapping at their bows. Tall apartment buildings hovered over them, affording what must have been amazing views of the harbor and killer sunrises each and every morning.

I had always wondered what it would be like to live near the water. Growing up in central Pennsylvania, I had never even been to the ocean. Now, seeing the Atlantic for the first time—even if it was just a tame inlet—I was hooked. It was all so peaceful and beautiful and serene.

"You look star struck," Whittaker said to me as he turned the car and put the harbor in the rearview mirror.

"It's just really nice," I said. "Thanks for bringing me."

Whittaker smiled. "Any time."

We zipped along the water past huge hotels and the state-of-the-art aquarium and I struggled to keep my mouth closed. I was actually in Boston. Home to Boston College and MIT, the Boston Bean and Boston cream pie, site of the infamous Tea Party and a million other historical events. Whittaker *could* really take me places.

The restaurant was tucked into a quaint neighborhood on the north side of the city, where brownstone buildings abounded and old-fashioned street lamps flickered over stone-covered streets. A tuxedoed valet took the keys to Whittaker's car and he offered his arm again as he led me through the door. A crumbling cornerstone near the sidewalk read 1787.

Once we were inside, another valet slipped my coat from my arms and a third led us to a table in the back corner, close enough to a roaring fire that we could enjoy its warmth, but far enough away that we wouldn't get overheated. The conversation in the room was hushed, accompanied by the sounds of tinkling china and silverware. As I sat in the cushioned chair, I tried not to stare at the diamonds that dripped from every female neck and wrist in the room. Never in my life had I been in a restaurant so elegant, surrounded by people for whom money was no object. *If my parents could see me now.*

"Mr. Whittaker. A pleasure to see you," a tall, mustached man greeted us. "Would you like to see the wine list?"

"That won't be necessary, John," Whit said. "We'll have a bottle of the Barolo '73 we had for my parents' anniversary."

I blinked. Wasn't there still a legal drinking age in this country?

"A fine choice, sir. Beth will be right over with your menu." He executed a slight bow and moved soundlessly away.

"No carding?" I asked.

Whittaker chuckled. "Reed, please."

All righty, then. I crossed my legs under the table, bonking the underside with my knee and causing all the dishes to jump.

"Oops. Sorry," I said.

"It's okay," Whittaker said in a quiet, soothing voice, the one that sent pleasant reverberations right through me. "Just relax."

"Right. Relax."

I rested my elbows on the table, then quickly yanked them away. Was the elderly woman at the next table glaring at me, or was that just the natural state of her face? Under the white tablecloth, I fiddled with the chunky gold bracelet Kiran had lent me. Luckily, Whittaker didn't seem to notice my continued fidgeting. He leaned back and smiled as a slim man in a black vest poured ice water into our glasses. For the first time, I noticed there were three stems of various sizes behind my plate. Apparently we were to do a lot of drinking. That led me to the ornate silverware, of which there was far too much. Two spoons, three forks, two knives. What could they possibly be used for?

"Would madam like a bit of bread?"

Suddenly another man was hovering over me, proffering a basket full of rolls. They smelled incredible and I could feel their warmth on my face.

"Uh . . . sure," I said, reaching for a brown bun.

The man cleared his throat and I froze. "If madam would like to select one, I would be happy to serve her," he said.

"Oh." My face flushed and I glanced at the old woman. Now I was *sure* she was glaring.

"I'll have the brown one, please," I said, utterly defeated.

"The pumpernickel? A fine choice," he said with a tight smile. Then he produced a pair of silver tongs from behind his back, plucked the roll from the basket, and placed it on my bread plate. No fair hiding the tongs. If I had seen them, I might have known.

"For you, sir?" he said, turning to Whittaker.

Once Whit had made his selection, the bread guy slid over to the wall, where he stood next to the water guy, just waiting to be summoned at any moment. I couldn't believe these were actual jobs. What did these men put on their résumés? Expert Starch Distributor? Professional Thirst Quencher?

As soon as the bread guy was free and clear, a pretty blonde stepped up and handed Whittaker a leather-bound menu.

"Welcome to Triviatta," she said. "My name is Beth. Please feel free to ask any questions."

"Thank you, Beth," Whittaker said, looking over the menu.

She turned and started off.

"Uh, Beth?" I said, stopping her in her tracks. "I have a question."

Several people turned to stare. Perhaps I had spoken too loudly.

"Yes, miss?" she asked, utterly confused.

"Can I have a menu?" I asked in a whisper. Both she and Whittaker just stared. The bread guy laughed and the water guy whacked the bread guy's leg. My face burned. "Oh. Sorry. Can I have a menu, please?"

Beth looked at Whittaker for direction. He smiled indulgently and nodded.

"One moment," Beth said.

She smiled tightly, eyeing me as if I was a dog off the street, begging for a free meal. When she finally walked off again, I leaned in toward Whittaker.

"Did I do something wrong?"

"Oh, no," Whittaker said. "I like that you're so . . . independent."

"Because I want my own menu?" I asked, my shoulder muscles coiling slightly.

"It's just, this place is old school," Whittaker told me. "Usually the man orders for the woman."

"Well, that's archaic."

"No. It's tradition," Whittaker corrected.

I felt like a five-year-old. Instantly, resentment took over. I didn't want to be here. I didn't *have* to be here. He had some gall, talking down to me that way. Beth returned with my menu and I opened it without thanking her. I scanned the list of meals quickly and ruled most of them out because they either 1) contained seafood, to which I was allergic, or 2) were unpronounceable. I closed the menu and placed it on the table.

"Decided already?" Whittaker said, lifting his eyebrows.

"Yes." My foot bounced up and down under the table.

"What would you like?" he asked.

"You really need to know?" I snapped.

He blinked. "If I'm going to order for us, I do."

"I can order for myself, thanks," I said.

Whittaker let out an impatient sigh that curled my toes. He slowly lowered his menu and looked at me almost sternly over the flickering candles.

"Reed, at least let me order for you," he said. "That's the way it's done here."

I stared at him. What kind of guy was he? This was the way he wanted to spend his eighteenth birthday? At a restaurant so old school my grandfather would have felt out of place? I couldn't believe that this was his idea of a good time.

"Whittaker, can I ask you a question?" I said, leaning forward.

"Of course," he said.

"Why are we here? Why aren't you out partying with Dash and Gage and those guys?" I said. "I'm sure they could have figured out something debaucherous for you to do tonight. I mean, isn't that what friends do on their friends' birthdays?"

Whittaker flinched ever so slightly and looked back down at his menu. He cleared his throat and made a big show of scanning the options. "Dash and Gage have . . . other things going on tonight," he said. "And besides, I told you, you're the only person I want to spend my birthday with."

In that moment it all became clear. It was a lie. All of it. It wasn't that he didn't want to hang out with Dash and Gage and Josh, but that they hadn't shown any interest in hanging out with *him*. For

all their bluster over how much they loved Whit, it was just that—
bluster. They found him amusing, but they weren't really his
friends. If they were, he *would* have been with them tonight.

I knew what that was like. I had spent plenty of birthdays with
no party, no friends, no one around but my brother and my father,
who had to be there, my mother an ever-ominous presence. There
was nothing worse, in my experience, than a miserable birthday.

With a deep breath, I made a decision. Old-fashioned or not,
condescending or not, Whittaker was basically a good guy. And he
deserved a good birthday. As of now, it was my job to make that
happen.

"I'll have the filet mignon, medium," I told him.

Whittaker smiled and sat up a bit straighter. "Good choice.
Appetizers? Dessert?"

"It's your birthday," I said. "Your night, your choice."

heartbreaker

"Yes! Another winner!" I cheered, raising my fists in the air as Whittaker pulled his car through the security gate at Easton. It was pitch-dark outside and the security guard waved us through without even looking up from his mini television. For the first time all evening I realized that I was reluctant for the night to end. Once I had relaxed and decided to treat the whole thing as a night out with a friend who just wanted a good birthday, I had actually started to have a good time.

"How much?" Whittaker asked gleefully.

"Two dollars and fifty cents," I said, holding up the scratch-off card. "Told you this was a good investment."

The entire car was littered with scratch-off lottery tickets. On the floor at my feet were dozens of useless cards, while stacked on my lap were the few winners. Five dollars here, twenty dollars there—it was all adding up.

"You may even make your money back," I told Whittaker, picking up the last card. He'd dropped a hundred dollars at the convenience store on the highway. The guy behind the counter had looked at us like we were nuts, but had patiently counted off one hundred of the tiny game cards.

"Lottery tickets. I never would have even thought of that," Whittaker said, downshifting as we climbed the winding hill.

"Really? This is the first thing everyone at home does on their eighteenth," I said. Of course, I guessed people like Whittaker never played the lottery. I should have been surprised that he even knew the lottery existed. I scratched off the last square. The symbol there didn't match any of the others. "Nothing," I said, tossing it on the floor.

"So, what's the final tally?" he asked.

I reached up and turned on the overhead light so I could see better. Quickly I flipped through our winning cards and did the math in my head. "One hundred two dollars and fifty cents," I announced. "You made a profit."

"Wow. Good for me," he said.

"You just have to take them to a lottery dealer to cash them in," I said, straightening the pile in my lap.

"You keep them," he said.

"What? No," I said. "These are your birthday tickets."

"Yes, but it was your idea," Whittaker said as he pulled the car into the circle that fronted Bradwell and the other underclassmen dorms. "I insist."

An unpleasant warmth spread through my chest. A hundred dollars. That was a lot of money. To me. Clearly, to him it was chump change. Throwing it out the window was no problem for him.

"Okay," I said finally. "Thanks."

He pulled the car to a stop at the curb and put it in park. Instantly the vibe in the car went from silly and celebratory to serious and loaded. This was it. The moment of truth. End of the date time. I had already decided hours earlier that if he tried to kiss me, I would let him. It was what he wanted, that much was obvious, and it would be a small price to pay for everything he had given me, everything he *could* give me. But now that the time had come I wondered if I could go through with it. The more time I spent with Whit, the fonder I was of him, but not in the way he wanted me to be.

He was more like a brother. The death knell when it came to romantic possibilities.

Whittaker cleared his throat. I turned to look at him. Okay. I could do this. It was just a kiss.

"Reed, I've been wondering," Whittaker said, rubbing his flat palm on the leg of his pants.

If you can kiss me? Sure. Go ahead. Get it over with.

"Would you do me the honor of being my date for the Legacy tomorrow night?"

"What?"

Just like that. The Golden Ticket. Tossed in my lap. Right at a moment I was dreading. I was so happy I almost laughed. But instead, I bit my lip.

"The Legacy. Everyone's going," Whittaker said, mistaking my surprise for actual confusion. "I'd like you to be my date."

"Sure. Absolutely," I said. "I'd love to."

Whittaker beamed. For a moment we just sat there and smiled and I thought that maybe, just maybe, he was feeling the same way I was. That this was just happy camaraderie. We really were just friends.

And then he grabbed my face roughly between both hands and kissed me.

Right. Maybe not.

I tried to suck in breath through my nose as Whittaker's mouth moved awkwardly over mine. Finally he pulled back, panting, and looked me in the eye. I took in as much oxygen as possible without making it obvious he had almost smothered me.

"I've wanted to do that all night," he said. "I know I said we could just be friends, but Reed, there's this attraction between us. We can't ignore it any longer."

Riiiiight.

Whittaker stared at me. He was waiting for me to say something. To agree with him. But I couldn't. I just couldn't lie to him about something like that. But I couldn't tell him the truth either— that I liked him, but not in *that* way. It would break his heart and I couldn't do that to him. Especially not on his birthday.

"I'm so glad you're going with me," he said finally.

All right. Enough was enough. I had to set this guy straight, even if it might mean losing out on this party, on seeing Thomas. I couldn't do this to him.

"Whit, I—"

A sudden knock on the window caused us both to jump. Whittaker stared past me.

"It's Mrs. Lattimer," he said.

"Oh, God." My heart slammed into my ribcage. How long had she been there? Had she watched us kiss?

"Here. Take this," Whittaker said, pressing something small and cold into my hand.

It was a necklace, a slim gold chain with a small ovular pendent. In the center of the oval was a tiny crown made out of itsy-bitsy diamonds.

"What is it?" I asked.

"You'll need it for tomorrow night," he replied. "Just put it away. Quick," he said, casting Mrs. Lattimer a furtive look.

Heart pounding, I tucked the necklace into my bag, then smoothed the loose hair behind my ears and straightened my skirt. I shot Mrs. Lattimer a quick, sheepish glance through the window and she responded with a tart, knowing look.

"Good evening, Miss Brennan," she said, holding her collar up tightly with one fist. "It's time to say good night."

Whittaker looked at me apologetically and then got out of the car. I shoved the lottery tickets in my pocket and gathered up my roses as he came around and opened the door for me. My knees quaked as I placed one high heel on the sidewalk. Whittaker saw the hesitation and basically pulled me to my feet.

"Good night, Reed," Whittaker said as Mrs. Lattimer backed up the slightest bit.

"Good night, Whit," I replied. "Happy birthday."

"Thank you," he said.

And then, much to my shock and, I'm sure, the shock of Mrs. Lattimer, he leaned in and gave me one last kiss. Closed mouthed, lingering, gentle.

"Ahem," Mrs. Lattimer said. She didn't even clear her throat. Merely stated the word.

Whittaker pulled away, smiled all gooey, and got back in his car. I turned and smiled awkwardly at Mrs. Lattimer.

"A successful night, then?" she said.

"You could say that," I told her, trying to quench the guilt. I hadn't had the chance to tell Whit how I really felt. Now he was going back to his dorm thinking he'd scored a second date. And even worse? Part of me was relieved. I really wanted to go to that damn party. I *had* to.

And, I mean, was it really so bad? Whittaker really wanted to go with me. He hadn't asked anyone else. What was wrong with accepting a good friend's invitation?

Ugh. I loathed myself.

"Come along," Mrs. Lattimer said. "It's very late."

I took a deep breath in an attempt to calm my nerves. Nerves from the kiss, from getting caught, from knowing that I was going to the Legacy and everything that meant to me, to Whit, to Thomas. I breathed in and looked up at the sky, but my gaze never got there. It stopped with a jolt at a window in the top floor of Bradwell. A window through which Missy, Lorna, and Constance were staring.

My already spastic heart now sank clear down through my abdomen and into my toes. Constance. She had seen it all. It was written all over her face. The car, the flowers, the kiss. Her heart was breaking as she sat there and stared. And I was the one who had broken it.

first impressions

I made the beds quickly on Saturday morning and raced out of Billings, hoping to catch Constance the moment she emerged from Bradwell. Once out on the quad I realized I hadn't been fast enough. Constance was already halfway to the cafeteria, flanked on one side by Kiki and Diana, on the other by Lorna and Missy. Like suddenly they were her best friends. Last week they couldn't have cared less about Constance, so I knew they were just aligning themselves with her because it meant standing up to me.

But I wasn't afraid of them. Compared to the people I had to deal with on a daily basis in my own home, these girls were teddy bears.

"Constance!" I shouted. There was a slight trip in her step. Lorna turned her head to look, then whispered something in Constance's ear. They all upped their pace. "Constance! Come on! Wait up!"

They didn't pause or even slow down. Luckily I could have caught them all even if I had a sprained ankle and a respirator. I jogged around and got in front of them. The look of pure hurt Constance cast my way was enough to take the breath out of me. They used that moment to move around me and keep walking.

"Constance!" I placed my hand on her shoulder. She whirled around, red hair flying.

"What?" she snapped. Her face was all blotchy and moist, her eyes psychotically bright green and rimmed with red.

"I . . . I'm sorry, all right?" I said.

Constance narrowed her eyes and shifted her weight from one foot to the other. "For what?" she asked, lifting her chin.

"For last night," I said. "I know you saw us and I swear I didn't want any of that to happen. You have to believe me."

"Right. You didn't want to go on an off-campus date with one of the hottest guys at Easton," Constance said. "You didn't want to get flowers. You didn't want to get *kissed*."

"Yeah. Sure looked that way to us," Missy said sarcastically.

I ignored her. She didn't matter.

"Constance, I'm telling you. I have no interest in Whittaker," I said.

"Oh, why? Is he not good enough for you?" Constance said, clearly offended. "Now that you're in Billings the guy that I've had a crush on my entire life is *beneath* you?"

"No! I didn't say that," I told her. But what could I say? There was no way to explain away what she had seen. And I had already resolved to keep seeing him, at least until tonight. Until the Legacy. What exactly was I trying to do here?

"Listen, I just . . . I wanted to say I was sorry," I told her finally. "That's all."

"Well, I'm sorry too," Constance said. She had tears in her voice but wouldn't let them out. "Sorry I ever thought I could trust you. Sorry I ever thought we could be friends."

Missy and Lorna both smirked and whispered to each other. Diana looked ill and Kiki just stared off toward the caf, listening to her iPod.

"You know, when I first met you I thought I had lucked out. I had this cool roommate, totally unaffected, totally nice," Constance said. "But that was all just an act, wasn't it? All you wanted from day one was to get into Billings and leave me behind. And now you're just as shallow and backstabbing as the rest of them."

Even Missy looked shocked at that. No one spoke badly of the Billings Girls. At least not anyone as low on the Easton food chain as Constance.

"Just goes to show you that first impressions mean nothing," Constance finished. "Come on, you guys."

She turned around and walked off, on some level enjoying the power she now wielded over the small group. Temporarily, of course. Until pitying her was no longer entertaining or fruitful. As I watched them go I realized the full implications of what I had done. Constance had been the only person who had liked me from day one, who had been there for me from day one, and who had expected nothing in return.

She'd had the potential, at least, to be a true friend. But I had killed that potential. Now, the Billings Girls were all I had left. If I was going to have any friends at Easton, any life at all, it was going to be them. They were it. They were all.

confession

I walked into Billings House with a determination I hadn't felt since that day in sixth grade when I had resolved to finally tell off my mother. Of course, that had all died away when I'd stormed into the house and found her passed out in a puddle of drool. This time, however, I wasn't going to let anything stop me. Not Natasha, not the images from that night with Whit that were burned on my brain. Nothing. I had a job to do and I was going to do it, whatever the consequences.

I caught a few disturbed looks from random Billings residents as I took the front stairs two at a time, but no one stopped me or even said hello, and soon I was once again standing in front of Noelle's door. I rapped loudly.

"Come in!"

"Hey. I have to talk to you about some—"

Okay. *That* might stop me. Noelle stood in the center of the room in a gorgeous black ball gown, helping Ariana step into an even more gorgeous aqua-colored frock. Ariana wore nothing but a thong and a strapless bra and her stomach was flatter than a paper plate. Neither one of them flushed, flinched, or paused as I entered the room.

"Hi, Reed," Ariana said with a small smile.

She let Noelle pull the dress up from the floor, and then slipped her arms through the skinny straps. Noelle zipped her up and there they stood, Noelle the vampy queen, Ariana the fairy princess. I had never seen dresses like these outside of the Oscars.

"Is . . . is that what you're wearing tonight?" I asked. Strewn on Noelle's bed were half a dozen masquerade masks in various colors, decorated with sequins, feathers, and beads.

"We're still deciding," Noelle said, turning to face her full-length mirror and swishing the full skirt back and forth. Meaning they had more such gowns stashed somewhere in this room? Why hadn't I found those in all my searches? "You said you had something to tell us?" she asked, her eyes meeting mine in the reflection.

Right. Focus time. Bite-the-bullet time. Perhaps duck-and-cover time.

"There's something I need to confess," I said, my heart fluttering. "And you're not going to like it."

Noelle and Ariana exchanged a glance. Ariana sat gracefully on the edge of the bed, tucking her skirt beneath her and crossing her legs at the ankle.

"Go on," she said.

"Where to start?" I said, looking at the ceiling and wiping my sweaty palms on my jeans.

"The beginning always seems a good place," Ariana said.

I laughed nervously. "Right. Okay, well. Remember that night out in the woods? At the end of parents' weekend? The night I met Whit?"

I swallowed hard.

"Yes," Noelle said, holding a diamond chandelier earring up to her ear.

"Well, that night, Natasha apparently took some pictures of me. And Whit. Doing things," I said.

That got their attention. Noelle finally turned away from the mirror and looked directly at me. I expected her to be shocked and appalled, but she simply smirked.

"What kind of things?" she said.

Oh, God. She was going to make me say it. Couldn't she see my skin was burning off over here? "Kissing, drinking. You know."

"Okay," Ariana said blankly.

"Well, she showed me the pictures and threatened to send them to the dean and have me kicked out of school unless . . . unless . . ."

They were going to kill me. They were going to tear my hair out and gouge my eyes and, worse, have me thrown out of Easton faster than you could say "nice try."

"Unless . . . ," Ariana prompted, waving a hand blithely in front of her.

"Unless I spied on you guys," I blurted finally, closing my eyes. "Well, not *spied* exactly, but snooped. Through your stuff. While I was supposed to be cleaning. She thinks that you guys got Leanne Shore kicked out of school and she wanted me to find proof."

I waited for the explosion, but none came. When I was finally able to focus again, Ariana was still staring at me. Noelle was still smirking. Where was the shock? The indignation? They should have been furious at me. Or at the very least surprised and angry at Natasha for trying to use me. But they just stood there. I had no idea what the hell was going on.

"And did you?" Noelle asked.

"Snoop or find proof?" I asked.

"Either. Both," Ariana said.

My head automatically bowed. "Yes. I did. I found something, but I haven't done anything with it. I swear."

I wished they would say something. Anything. I *wished* they would yell and scream. They were silent as monks. And it was far more disturbing than any freak-out could ever be.

"Well, anyway, here's what I found," I said, whipping the disk out of my back pocket and holding it out. Neither one of them moved. Finally I had to step past Noelle and place the disk on her desk. Then I backed up to my spot and waited. And waited. This was torture of the most brutal kind. "So . . . what're you going to do?"

Noelle sighed dramatically. She turned around and lifted another earring out of a box. "Nothing."

"What do you mean, nothing?" I said. Although I knew I had no right to, I was starting to get a little angry. Couldn't they see how difficult this was for me? Couldn't they see the future-threatening

predicament I was in? They could at least react in some way.
"Aren't you mad?"

"Not especially," Ariana replied, standing. She floated past me
over to her side of the room and removed a pair of silver sandal-
like shoes from the floor of her closet.

"But . . . what about Natasha?" I said, a swirling mire of desperation opening inside my chest. "If I tell her I gave that to you,
she's going to send those pictures. I'm going to get kicked out."

"Stop whining," Noelle said. "It doesn't become you."

She fastened an earring into her ear and then turned around,
regarding me with an almost pitying smile.

"Wait—," I started to protest.

Noelle brought her hands up to her lips. "Sssshhh," she said,
in an almost comforting way. "Look, just forget about that for right
now, okay?" And then she smiled. "Now, did Whittaker ask you to
the Legacy or not?" she said.

What the hell did that have to do with anything?

"Yes."

"Good," Noelle said. "He gave you the necklace?"

"Yeah. What's that about?" I asked.

"You have to wear it. It's your pass to get in," Noelle said.

Damn. Whoever heard of a party where the proof of invitation
was a solid-gold-and-diamond necklace? Who paid for this stuff?

"Let's do this." Noelle nodded over my shoulder at Ariana, who
reached into her closet and pulled out an incredible, shimmering
gold gown in a clear bag. A gold mask with a white feather across

one side hung from the silver hanger. She draped the dress across one arm and brought it over, holding it out to me. The gown took my breath away, even as the rest of me was still reeling from everything else.

"That's for me?" I said.

"Kiran guessed your measurements," Ariana explained.

"Girl has a ninety-nine point nine percent success rate," Noelle said. "It's a talent."

"I don't believe this," I told them, overwhelmed.

Noelle shrugged. "I called in a favor at Roberto Cavalli. You can't exactly go to the Legacy in jeans and a T-shirt." She looked me up and down, amused. "We'll talk about this later." She turned around and lifted her thick mane of hair. "Unzip me?"

I hesitated. "You're getting *un*dressed?"

"It's not like we sneak off campus in ball gowns, Reed. That would be a little too conspicuous," she said.

"Oh."

I reached out and unzipped her dress from the top all the way down her back. She stepped out of the gown, completely naked, and walked slowly over to her closet to slip into her silk robe. As she turned around I caught a glimpse of her angry red stomach scar. She didn't seem to be in a hurry to hide it—or anything else for that matter.

"Take it," Ariana said, holding the gold dress up.

"Yeah. Then go see if Kiran has any shoes that will match," Noelle said, then laughed. "I think it's safe to assume she does."

Gingerly, I took the dress from Ariana's arms. She smiled at me in a proud way. Like she was a mother dressing her little tomboy for the prom. I had no idea what to say. I knew I should thank them, but how was I going to walk out of here with absolutely nothing resolved?

"But—"

"We'll *talk* about it *later*," Noelle repeated firmly. "Now go. We only have an hour before it gets dark."

I had a feeling that one more moment's hesitation would push her over the edge, and as of now I was getting off relatively easy. So I took the dress and left, just hoping that somehow, some way, all of this would just work itself out.

weirdness

An hour and a half later, as the Amtrak train zipped through rural and suburban towns, blurring by trees and steeples and schools and parks, I understood what Noelle had meant when she said they hadn't decided what they were wearing yet. It meant that all the Easton girls who were going were gathered in the back of the train car, slipping in and out of gowns, passing them around, trying them on, giggling and flashing their skimpy underwear for all the men to see. They did this while I sat alone in a double seat in my gold dress, my Legacy necklace securely fastened, avoiding Natasha for dear life, wondering how I had ever gotten here.

"Yeah, baby! Take it off!" Gage shouted toward the back of the car, whooping it up with Dash. A silk thong came flying over and hit him in the face, accompanied by a round of girlish laughter. Dash passed Gage a flask of liquor as Gage pocketed the lingerie. He took a swig of vodka, never taking his lascivious eyes off the show.

"And you didn't want to take the train," he said to Dash mockingly.

Dash smirked. "I can admit when I'm wrong."

"Don't feel like playing dress-up?"

I looked up to find Josh standing in the aisle, one hand on the back of my seat, one hand on the back of the seat in front of me. He looked adorable in his black tuxedo, his curls as unruly as ever.

"I'm fine with what I have," I said, lifting the gold mask from my lap by its gold handle. I had changed into my gown in the tiny square of a bathroom the moment I boarded the train and I wasn't taking it off for anything. Never in my life had I even imagined wearing anything this divine.

"Good. I'm fine with it, too," he said. I smiled and felt myself blush. "May I?"

"Sure."

I was all too happy to have Josh sit with me. It would prevent Whittaker from taking the seat when he was done debating the latest Supreme Court debacle with the other guys from his floor. The ones who had either seen all the naked girls they needed to see or who didn't swing that way.

"So, you don't get a plus-one?" I asked as he settled in.

"Nope. I'm lucky I'm even here," he said with a shrug. "I'm third generation. Just made the cut."

"Ah."

"But look at you! You bagged one of the few plus-ones in the entire school. You must be so proud," he teased. "Not that I'm surprised."

"What do you mean?" I asked, not sure if I should be offended.

"Just that of all the girls in school I'm not surprised Whittaker picked you," he said.

I flushed with pleasure. So not offended.

"I don't even know if I'd bring someone if I *had* a plus-one," Josh said. "Unless I found someone truly worthy, I'd still go stag. That's just how I roll."

I laughed and shook my head. "The girls at school would eat you alive."

"So be it," he said. "So, how are you, Reed Brennan?"

I took a deep breath. "Fine. I'm fine."

"Convincing," he said with a facetious nod. "Keep saying that and even you might start to believe it."

I smiled sadly, snagged. "Do you really think Thomas is going to be at this thing?"

Josh faced forward and blew out a sigh, puffing his cheeks out momentarily. He picked at a slit in the back of the seat in front of him. "I hope so. So I can kick his ass."

I looked at him quizzically.

"You know, for making us worry," he said.

"Ah. Right. That tiny offense."

We looked at each other for a moment and I found myself staring directly into his green eyes—his kind, honest, nothing-to-hide green eyes. Slowly, Josh smiled, and I found myself smiling too. Then his gaze traveled down and settled, for the briefest of seconds, on my lips.

And just like that, my heart flipped.

Flipped. For Josh Hollis.

I looked away quickly, suddenly warm. Josh instantly did the same. Thomas. I was going to this party to see Thomas. Of course, Whittaker chose that very moment to finally arrive.

My head was spinning.

"Evening, Josh," he said congenially. "It seems you're in my seat."

My stomach clenched with nerves as Josh looked at me. I shrugged with my eyes. "See you later?" Josh said as he stood, Whittaker backing up to make room.

"Yeah."

Whittaker sat down next to me and slung his heavy arm around my shoulder. "This is going to be an incredible night."

"Yeah," I replied, toying with my masquerade mask as I stared at Josh over the top of the seat. He was talking to Gage and Dash now, laughing as if nothing was weird. "Yeah, it definitely is."

walk of fame

By the time we stepped off the train in Grand Central Station in New York, almost everyone was sufficiently wasted, so I wasn't that surprised when Kiran and Taylor came up behind me, hooked their arms through mine, and dragged me through the main lobby, laughing and whispering, drunk with absolute freedom. Our voices echoed off the incredible domed ceiling high above as we scurried along, trying not to trip over our gowns. I couldn't believe I was in New York City, center of the known universe. But even more shocking? I was there with these people, in an exquisite ball gown, earning the curious and awed stares of everyone around us.

I felt like a debutante, a celebrity, someone who was certainly not me.

"Where are we going?" I asked the moment we emerged clumsily onto the sidewalk, a six-legged princess in too-high heels.

The rest of the crowd brought up the rear, gabbing loudly and confidently, not caring who heard or who stared. The cars on the avenue raced by, honking and veering and slamming their brakes. A hot dog vendor pushed his cart along the curb, cursing at no one and everyone. A pack of kids in Spider-Man and Bratz costumes scurried after a pair of harried-looking moms. Two huge men in black leather jackets screamed insults at each other as they plowed right through our group, causing Rose and Cheyenne to jump out of their way. Five seconds in the city and already I had seen more hustle and bustle than I had during a lifetime in Croton, Pennsylvania.

"You'll see!" Kiran trilled, dragging me off down the sidewalk.

A pack of college-aged kids in elaborate vampire robes and white powder glided by us, checking us all out. A tall guy in a monkey costume gripped hands with a beautiful girl dressed up like Naomi Watts from *King Kong* and pulled her across the street. Ghouls and goblins shouted out taxi windows and a limo went by with four guys shoved up through the sunroof, each dressed in drag with tremendous boobs, "Woo-wooing" at the top of their lungs.

"Love New York on Halloween," Noelle said, taking a drink from a flask. "It's when all the crazies come out."

We walked a few blocks, making a few turns, until my feet started to throb in Kiran's wicked-high heels and I began to wonder why these ridiculously rich kids hadn't hired a limousine or at least hailed a cab. But the longer we walked, and the more passersby stopped in awe, the more I understood. They wanted these people to see and admire them. That was what this walk was all about. It was their walk of fame.

And it was fine by me, pain or no pain, because I got to see the city. I did my best not to gape as we strolled by swank boutiques and canopied restaurants. Tried so hard not to stare through the brightly lit windows into brownstone mansions, some starkly decorated with white walls and high ceilings, others jam-packed with overflowing bookcases and antique artifacts. Didn't even flinch when we traipsed past a woman pushing a stroller who might or might not have been Sarah Jessica Parker and who may or may not have paused to admire my gown. But I did take it all in. I took it all in and filed it away and told myself over and over that I belonged here. That I was not going to wake up. That all this was really happening. To me.

We emerged onto a wide avenue with islands down the center that were full of trees and bushes. A middle-aged couple in evening wear glided by us, the woman's silk skirt swishing behind her as she walked, her humongous diamond-and-ruby earrings sparkling under the streetlights. I surreptitiously glanced at the street sign over my head, trying not to seem too bumpkin, and smiled. We were on Park Avenue. *The* Park Avenue. It actually existed and I, Reed Brennan, was on it.

"This way!" Dash announced, leading the pack across the street.

I passed by an idling Rolls-Royce and tried not to stare at the uniformed driver as Kiran, Taylor, and I fell into a rhythm with our steps. We followed the others up the street as I glanced into each and every lobby, noting the elaborate marble floors, glistening chandeliers, gorgeous flower arrangements. I was completely dumbstruck by all the opulence, and Kiran and Taylor were having fun listening to the *clip-clop* of our heels—so much fun that we almost walked right by the rest of our friends when they stopped, en masse, in front of a wrought-iron gate. Apparently we had arrived.

Dash hit a buzzer that was built into a gray stone wall, and two seconds later an imposing man in a green doorman's uniform with gold tassels appeared. He looked us over with disdain, as if we were rabble off the street.

"Can I *help* you?" he said through his nose.

Noelle stepped up, nearly shoving Dash aside. The doorman had the humanity, at least, to appear stunned by the gorgeousness that had appeared in front of him. His eyes trailed down to the spot just above her cleavage, where her own Legacy pendant glimmered.

The man's thin lips twisted into a smile and he bowed his head. "Welcome."

He unlocked the gate, which gave an ages-old squeal. Dash flashed his sleeves, showing off a pair of Legacy cuff links—the guys' version of a pass—and the man bowed to him as well. Whittaker took my hand, detaching me from my friends, and showed his cuff links as we passed. The doorman glanced at my chest and nodded and my skin sizzled with excitement. I was in. My plus-one had been rendered. Now it was time to get to the task at hand.

the welcome

"This place is unbelievable," I whispered to Whittaker as we wove our way through the milling guests. His hand was hot and sweaty and practically crushing mine. All I wanted to do was stop and take a look around, but Whittaker was in a rush to get who knew where.

"Come on. We have to get a good spot for the welcome," he said, hurrying me along.

I held my mask up with my trembling free hand, struggling to see in the candlelight. I would have taken it down, but everyone else seemed intent on wearing theirs, and I didn't want to look like the gawker I was.

"The welcome?"

Whittaker didn't reply. It was so dark I could barely make out the faces around me, especially with my line of sight partially impaired by sequins. If the lighting remained this way throughout the party, I would never be able to spot Thomas. Especially not if he was wearing a mask, like everyone else was. My only hope was that Thomas would choose to be different. Not a bad bet, actually.

All around me skirts swished, drinks were sipped, hushed voices murmured. For the party of the century, it was quite tame at the moment. I scanned the crowd and saw no one familiar, not even the people I had come with. Everyone had dispersed the second we stepped off the elevator, disappearing within the sea of hidden faces.

Finally Whittaker paused near a wall and I was able to take a breath. He whispered something to a tall, skinny waiter, who returned momentarily with two drinks on a tray. Whittaker handed me an extremely pink beverage in a frosted martini glass and took the short, dark snifter for himself. I attempted to hold the glass with one hand and sloshed some of the liquid over the side onto the exquisite marble floor. Apparently I needed some practice.

Decision time. Take off the mask or make a complete mess? I tucked my mask under my arm so I could hold the drink with both hands.

"Who lives here?" I asked.

"The Dreskins," Whittaker said, unfazed as he surveyed the dozens of coutured legacies milling about the great room. "Donald Dreskin, Dee Dee Dreskin, and their parents. They're good friends of the family."

"Oh. So you've been here before?" I asked.

"On occasion," he said. "And every year for this. The Dreskins have been hosting the Legacy since before I was born."

He was so incredibly blasé about the whole thing. As if every day he was whisked up to the two-floor penthouses of Park Avenue buildings in private elevators that required special keys to work. As if this apartment, which stretched the entire span of the building on both floors and was bigger than my entire house times five, was just another home. So far all I had seen was the wide-open foyer with its story-high Picassos and its deco chandelier, followed by this humongous room with its windows overlooking Central Park—*the* Central Park—and I was ready to faint with awe.

Suddenly there was a distinct murmur throughout the crowd as everyone turned in our direction. I glanced over my shoulder to see what the fuss was about and saw that the two grand doors behind me were opening. The floor on that side of the room was raised three steps, creating a sort of stage.

"Ah. Here we are," Whittaker said expectantly.

Through the doors stepped a tall man in a tuxedo, wearing a wooden mask of a grotesque, leering clown face. He clasped his hands in front of him and everyone fell silent.

"Welcome one, welcome all," the man said, his voice only slightly muffled by the mask. "As the master of ceremonies for this year's Legacy it is my honor, my privilege, to invite each and every one of you into the inner sanctum." There was a sizzle of anticipation felt even by me, although I had no idea what was going on. The master raised one finger in warning. "But remember, what you see here . . . what you do here . . . who you touch here . . . who you screw here . . ."

Knowing laughter all around.

"*All* will remain here," he said. "For this is the Legacy, my friends. You are the chosen. So make your peace now with whomever you worship, and never . . . look . . . back."

With that, the master stepped aside and everyone moved to the doors at once as if an emergency evacuation had been called.

"What's in there?" I asked Whittaker as he tugged at my hand. After that speech, I was feeling more than a little wary.

"You'll see," Whittaker said with a mischievous smile.

His grip on my hand tightened as we neared the double doors and I wondered, for the first time, if I might have gotten myself in over my head.

dance, dance

Walking through the doors was like going through the looking glass. A tremendous ballroom had been draped from ceiling to floor with swags of red, black, pink, and purple velvet and chiffon. Ropes of sparkling mirrors dangled everywhere, catching the strobe lights and sending prisms over the hundreds of masked faces. Acrobats hung from cloth ropes tied to the ceiling, twirling and whirling over our heads, their barely clad bodies painted in swirls of color. In the center of the room, most of the partygoers were already starting to dance to the deafening beat being laid down by a DJ in the far corner. On a circular stage next to him, a small orchestra played a frenzied song, their music intertwining with the beat to form some seriously eerie, exotic, almost frantic music. Gorgeous women in elaborate costumes circulated around the room, offering drinks and ushering people behind curtained-off areas.

My head spun. There was too much going on around me. Too much mayhem, too much activity. Just too much.

"Reed!"

Kiran appeared out of nowhere and grabbed my hand. "Come dance!" she shouted.

I looked at Whittaker, who waved me off. "Go!"

"I'll find you!" I said. At the moment he seemed like the one and only solid thing in my life.

"Or I'll find you," he promised.

Then, for the hundredth time that night, I let Kiran drag me away. We passed by a large opening like a coat-check room, where a tall woman dressed like an angel was handing out gifts of various sizes, wrapped in white paper. A pack of girls took their gifts and rushed off to an alcove with them.

"What are they doing?" I asked.

"The white gift. The Legacy's answer to favors," Kiran said over her shoulder. "Nothing worth less than a thousand."

"A thousand dollars?" I said, gaping.

"Yeah, but you still never get what you want," Kiran shouted. "The swap party happens later."

Unbelievable. This party was unbelievable. Who knew there was this much wealth in the world?

Finally, Kiran somehow found Noelle, Dash, Ariana, Taylor, and Gage on the dance floor and dove right in, twirling me around once before letting me go and leaving me to my own devices. I had never been much of a dancer and for a moment I was self-conscious, until I really took a look around me and saw how everyone else was doing. Suffice it to say, there wasn't really anyone to impress. I closed my eyes, lifted my arms, and let myself go.

Cathartic. That was the only word to express the feeling. The longer I danced, the more all I had been through, all I anticipated going through, faded into the background. The music was so loud it seemed as if it was coming out of my bones, through my pores, reverberating from my own body and crowding out everything else.

This was perfection. Yes, perfection. Insulated in the center of the dance floor. Insulated from Whittaker and those alcoves and whatever might be going on within them. Insulated from Natasha and her threats, from Constance and her accusations, from Thomas and his betrayal and the worry that surrounded every thought of him. This was my comfort zone. If I could just stay here among my friends for the rest of the night, I would be fine.

"Having fun?" Noelle shouted, twirling over and throwing her arms around my neck. She moved against me, completely sure, completely un-self-conscious. I did my best to mimic her movement, her confidence.

"Definitely."

"Good. You need this," Noelle said.

"What?" I asked. I had heard her, but had no idea what she meant.

"You need this!" she repeated, looking me in the eye. "Enjoy it!"

I missed a beat and bumped her hip. She smiled, turned, and shimmied back to Dash. Was it just me, or did her "enjoy it" have a "while you can" implied?

Oh, God. They *were* angry with me for giving in to Natasha's blackmail. They were going to let me fry. Tonight was some kind of mercy mission. Some kind of last hurrah. They were letting me see into the very core of their privileged world, into the Legacy, just so that it would be that much more painful when they snatched it all away.

I turned around, feeling suddenly ill, and looked around for a window, a balcony, any place where I might be able to find some air. And that was when I saw him and the entire room tilted beneath me.

Thomas.

double mindfreak

"Reed! Reed! Where're you going!?" Taylor shouted after me.

I didn't respond. Couldn't. There was no time. I elbowed my way through the gyrating bodies on the dance floor, stepping on toes and earning shoves and curses along the way. Strobe lights flashed, arms distorted my view, but I kept my eyes trained on him like a sniper on a hostile target. He was standing right there, sipping a drink, with one hand in his pocket. If he turned just slightly to the left, he would be looking right at me.

If he saw me, would he run? Would he approach? Why wouldn't he look my way?

"Thomas!" I screamed.

I was just arriving at the edge of the dance floor when he turned, lifted one of the dark curtains, and disappeared behind it. I grabbed up my skirt and ran, sidestepping a couple who was making out near one of the bars, ducking as an acrobat came dangerously close to impaling herself on one of my bobby pins. Gasping for breath, I whipped the curtain aside and there he was, standing with his back to me. I grabbed his shoulder and whipped him around.

"Thomas!" I gasped, barely audible.

It wasn't Thomas at all. The guy turned his startled brown eyes on me and quickly ducked out of the alcove as if he'd been caught with his hand in the cookie jar. He was too tall, his hair too long. He looked nothing like Thomas. How could I have ever mistaken him?

My heart pounded in my chest. I looked up from the floor—my eyes bleary and confused—and instantly all the air whooshed out of my lungs. For the first time I noticed that I was not alone. I noticed the reason the Thomas look-alike had bolted so quickly in obvious guilt.

There, in the corner, with her leg wrapped over another girl's lap, her hands entangled in another girl's blond hair, her tongue searching another girl's mouth, was none other than Natasha Crenshaw.

"Oh, my God," I said loudly.

Natasha turned around, heaving for breath, and for the first time I saw clearly the face of the girl beneath her—the chubby cheeks, the heavy makeup, the kiss-bruised lips of Leanne Shore.

blackmail boomerang

"Oh, this is just perfect," Leanne said sourly.

Yep. Just as pleasant as I remembered her.

"I'm so sorry," I said, backing away. "I thought I saw someone come in here and—"

Natasha swung her legs down and straightened her skirt. She pushed her hands into her knees, took a deep breath, and stood. Her breasts heaved in her straight-cut strapless dress and she yanked it up under her arms to cover a bit more of her cleavage.

"I'll just go," I said, feeling threatened.

"Don't," Natasha said.

I froze. There were about a hundred thousand places I would have rather been just then, but I couldn't move.

"You can't tell anyone about this, Reed," Natasha said, a plea in her voice. "Please. I know you pretty much hate me, and with good reason, but I'm begging you. Don't tell a soul."

I swallowed hard and looked from her to Leanne, who was averting her eyes, her hands flattened on the chaise at her sides.

Was Natasha begging me? Had she really just admitted I had reason to hate her? Natasha "Do-As-I-Say-or-Die" Crenshaw?

"I won't," I said. "I swear."

Natasha sighed and looked at the floor.

"Are you two . . . going out?" I asked.

Natasha and Leanne exchanged a long glance. Finally Natasha sat back down next to Leanne, her crinoline rustling. They stared into each other's eyes. Outside the music continued to pound.

"Go ahead," Leanne said finally, deflating. She leaned back against the wall and crossed her arms over her stomach. "Go ahead and tell her. She should know what they're really about."

Why did I have a feeling that this was going to make a little *more* sense than I needed it to?

Natasha lifted Leanne's hand and laced their fingers together. She looked up at me and nodded. "Yes. We're a couple," she said flatly. "We've been together since sophomore year."

"That's why you made me sneak around," I said, sitting on a bench across from them. "That's why you wanted Leanne back so badly."

Natasha tipped her head forward and sighed. "Reed, the blackmail was all a setup. I wasn't really blackmailing you. Noelle was blackmailing *me.*"

I shook my head slightly as this piece of information attempted to penetrate. "Excuse me. I think I just got whiplash," I said. "*What*?"

"They *told* me to take those pictures, Reed," Natasha said, leaning forward. "They told me to blackmail you."

I felt like one of the acrobats had just swooped in, tossed my feet over my head, and dropped me back down to the floor. I stared at the wall between Natasha and Leanne and tried to suck in a breath. Tiny black dots marred my vision and I closed my eyes against a wave of swirling nausea.

"Are you okay?" Natasha asked.

I placed my cool and clammy hand against my hot-as-fire forehead. "Why? Why? Wh—" It was the only word I could form. I opened my eyes and attempted to focus on Natasha. "Why would you do this to me?"

"Because they threatened to tell everyone about us," Natasha said, glancing at Leanne.

"So . . . what? You were afraid of being disowned by your Republican parents? Is that it?" I asked.

"No! It wasn't for me," Natasha said. "My parents know I'm a lesbian. I've been out with them since I was thirteen. They think it's cool. Like it gives them edge or something."

"So why?" I asked. "I don't understand."

"She did it for me, okay?" Leanne shouted. "God, how thick can you be? If my parents found out about us, I would be out on the street like that," she said, snapping her fingers. "They would not only disown me, they would destroy me. I would be lucky to get a job at the freakin' Gap, okay? She did it for me."

I felt my mouth hanging open. I stared as Natasha leaned back and touched Leanne's face gently with the back of her hand. Leanne drew in a shaky breath and quickly wiped back a tear.

Then they kissed. Slowly, tenderly, comfortingly. When they pulled away, Natasha touched her forehead to Leanne's and they both breathed.

This was not just a couple. This was a couple in love.

And as I realized this, I completely forgave Natasha. She had done it all for love, just as I had kept Thomas's note a secret, just as I had kept alive the hope that I would see him here tonight. Plus she had done it under threat from Noelle, and if there was one thing all three of us knew, it was that Noelle made good on her threats. Natasha, like me, had been given no choice.

I took a deep breath and tried to lock on to one coherent thought, tried to figure out what I had to do next, what I might need to know in order to do what I had to do next. There was one obvious question to be asked.

"Why would they do this?" I asked, gripping the soft cushion at my sides. "Why would they blackmail you to get me to sneak around their rooms? They had to know I would be screwed if I got kicked out. They had to know I would do it. I mean, you should have seen some of the embarrassing crap I found. Weren't they worried about that at all?"

"Maybe you should ask them," Leanne said flatly.

"She's right. You'll have an easier time believing it if it comes directly from them," Natasha said.

I nodded, still semicatatonic from the shock. Hear it from them. Right. They did have a lot of explaining to do.

"Would you mind leaving us alone now?" Leanne asked,

holding Natasha's hand in her lap. "We don't get to see each other much anymore."

She said this with a hint of blame. As if it was my fault. But I suppose, in a way, it was.

"Yeah. Sorry," I said, rising shakily on my three-and-a-half-inch heels. I paused in front of the curtain and looked over my shoulder at Natasha. "And don't worry. Your secret's safe."

Natasha smiled. The first genuine smile she had ever graced me with. "Thanks, Reed."

I lifted the curtain and ducked out.

the pawn

Why? Why would they do this? Why, why, why?

I paused for a moment outside the alcove to catch my breath, the boning in the bodice of my gown cutting into my raw, hot skin. My brain searched for an answer, but could find none. What would the Billings Girls possibly have to gain from making me snoop through *their* rooms? Had they wanted me to find all their sick, secret stashes? Had they wanted me to find the proof of what they had done to Leanne? And if so, I was back to question one:

Why?

It was all just some big, twisted game. It had to be. And Natasha and Leanne and I were the pawns. Playing with us amused them. Seeing how far we might go gave them a happy little thrill. It was the only explanation. Earlier that day when I had gone in and confessed and handed back the disk, they had known what I had done. They had known all along. They had engineered the whole thing.

They must have been laughing at me behind my back for days. *Look what Reed's doing. Look how stupid she is. Look how much power we have over her.*

The more I thought about it, the more I wanted to tear someone's hair out.

I stood up straight, took a deep breath, and homed in on the
dance floor. This was not going to be pretty.

Clinging to my livid adrenaline rush, I stormed through the
crowd, taking an elbow here, a hip knock there, and found Noelle,
Ariana, Taylor, and Kiran just where I had left them, in the center
of the dance floor. I stepped in front of Noelle, seething for
breath. She stopped dancing.

"We need to talk," I said.

"Reed, relax," she drawled, resting her wrists on my shoulders. "It's a party! That's what you're supposed to do. Or don't
they have parties in Bumblefuck, Pennsylvania?"

I grabbed her wrists, flung one away, and grasped the other
with my fingers. Tightly. Instantly I felt Ariana, Kiran, and Taylor
gather around me. I was surrounded, caged in, but I didn't care.

"We *need* to talk," I said again, this time through my teeth.

Noelle's eyes widened. "Reed, you're making a scene."

"I can make a much bigger, much louder one," I told her. "But
I really don't think you want all these people to hear the things I
have to say."

Noelle stared at me for a long moment, gauging whether or not
I was bluffing. I was. Totally. If I started ranting and raving, then I
would not only expose Leanne and Natasha's secrets, but I would
expose myself as a total naïve weakling. Not something I was quite
ready to do.

I narrowed my eyes. The longer we stood there, the more I realized I was winning. I could see her start to cave. Maybe two *could* play at this game.

"Fine," she said, ripping her hand from my grasp. "No need to get violent." She looked over my shoulder at the others. "Ladies. Let's find ourselves a room."

no more secrets

"Well, Reed, we're all here," Noelle said, lowering herself onto a large velvet chair in one of the alcoves. She kicked off her shoes and drew her feet up under her full skirt, as if she were settling in for a cup of tea and a long, pleasant chat. The others gathered around her on footstools and chaises.

It was all perfectly calm and civilized. A tableau of beautiful, poised, privileged women. Meanwhile, my insides were boiling.

"I know what you did," I said, standing in front of them. "I know you blackmailed Natasha into blackmailing me."

Noelle stared at me. "So what do you want, a medal?"

My fingers curled at my sides. "I want to know why," I said. "Why would you do that to me? What could you possibly have to gain?"

Noelle took a deep breath and sighed, looking off to her left like she was just that bored.

"It's not what *we* have to gain, so much as what *you* have to gain," Ariana said, reposing languidly on her chaise. Everyone watched me expectantly, as if waiting for me to thank them.

"What does that mean?" I asked. "I don't understand what that means."

"It means that we were testing you, and you passed!" Kiran announced grandly. She pulled her ever-present flask out of her purse and held it up. "Care to celebrate?"

I closed my eyes against a new wave of frustration. I was even more confused now than I'd been when I walked in here.

"Testing me? How? For what?" I asked.

Kiran took a long drink and touched her fingertips to her lips. Noelle shook her head, fed up. Ariana simply stared.

"To see if we could trust you," Taylor said quietly, looking at the floor. Her feet were turned in at the toes, giving the impression of a child waiting for her mother at the bus stop. "We did it to see if we could trust you."

To see if they could trust me. To see if they could *trust me*?

"And I passed? How is that possible?" I said. "I *did* go through your rooms. I found all kinds of crazy, personal crap. I totally violated your privacy. How did I pass?"

Noelle laughed. "You didn't violate anything. We planted all that stuff for you to find."

"*What?*" Okay. Now I had to sit. I dropped onto the nearest velvet bench and slumped. The past few weeks of my life passed before me in the blink of an eye. Had any of it been real? "Please tell me you're kidding."

"You really think I'm a closet binger?" Kiran said, snorting. "Please. I eat what I want, when I want. It's called good genes."

"Yeah. That was all my idea," Taylor said with obvious pride.

"But Taylor's all-work-and-no-play diary was mine," Kiran pointed out. "That was genius, you have to admit."

"It *was* good," Taylor said. "But I had finger cramps for days."

"The pictures of Dash were real, however. Unretouched," Noelle said with a satisfied smile. "I'm a lucky girl, aren't I?"

I tasted bile in the back of my throat. Not only had they set me up, they had gone to elaborate lengths to do so. This must have taken days to plan and execute. All along they had been plotting and scheming behind my back. I had thought they were my friends, but they had been messing with me from day one. Was anything any of them had ever said to me true?

"I'll never forget your face that first morning after Natasha showed you the slide show," Kiran said mirthfully. "On my birthday? Every time we handed you another gift you looked more and more green."

"That was such perfect timing," Ariana said. "You really laid on the guilt," she added with obvious pride.

"Honestly, I'm kind of surprised you didn't figure it out," Noelle told me. "We almost tripped up so many times."

"Like, oh my God, that morning I found you in our room? I was so not supposed to be there," Taylor said. "I totally forgot you would be sneaking around, but when I saw you I could tell you'd already been under my bed. And then I threw in that thing about my paper and you were *so* sweet. '*Everyone here says you're the smartest person ever to go here,*'" she said, mimicking my words. Words I had thought would help her. "That was so nice of you, Reed!"

"And then all that crap about passwords?" Kiran said. "We totally fed you the info on how to find Ariana's key."

"But my planner must have driven you crazy," Ariana said. "Sorry about that."

Never in my life had I felt humiliation so intense. They had known the entire time. They had been *leading me on*. That night when Ariana had handed me her bag, she had done it on *purpose*. I hadn't been clever or conniving or stealth. I had been duped.

"Anyway, the real test was whether or not you would turn us in if you found something incriminating," Noelle said. "If we threatened to take away your entire world—i.e., your enrollment at Easton—and you still remained loyal to us, you would pass."

"And you did," Ariana said simply. "Now we know we can trust you with anything. Everything."

A chill skittered over my skin and I wrapped my arms around myself. I couldn't believe this was happening. All that fear, all that sneaking, all that guilt. It was all for nothing.

"What would you have done if I'd gone directly to the dean with that disk?" I asked, staring at the floor. "It's kind of a dangerous game you were playing, isn't it? You could have gotten thrown out of school. All of you."

Noelle laughed again and this time was joined by the others. "Please, Reed. They'd need a lot more than that to kick *us* out of school. Danger? No. There was never any danger."

"Except for you," Kiran said, pointing at me. "For *you* there was danger. If those pictures had gotten out, you would have been on a bus back to Croton before you could say 'See ya.'"

"They really are quite incriminating," Noelle added matter-of-factly.

I pressed my hands into the bench at my sides and leaned forward, fighting back some serious nausea as they laughed. This was funny to them. It was all very amusing, toying with people's feelings. With their lives. With their futures.

"Oh, Reed, come on," Ariana said, standing. She glided over and sat down next to me, wrapping one arm around my shoulders and touching my wrist with her other hand. Her fingers were ice cold. "It's all good now. It's going to be okay. Don't you realize what all of this means?"

It means you're all nuts. It means you're all evil. It means I've aligned myself with the devil's minions.

"It means you're one of us now," Ariana said quietly. "Really and truly."

"It means you don't have to play Cinderella anymore," Taylor said.

"Which kind of sucks, because I hate making my own bed," Kiran added, taking another swig.

"It means you're in," Noelle stated simply. "For real this time. From here on out. No more secrets."

Something about these three words sent a thrill of excitement through my heart. Even in all my mind-twisting, stomach-clenching desperation, I was still psyched at the idea of actually being accepted by these nutcases. What was *wrong* with me?

I had been seduced. It was official. There was no turning back now. I finally looked up and met Noelle's dark eyes from across the room.

"No more secrets?" I said.

"None."

I took a deep breath and looked at Ariana. She gazed back with that enigmatic smile. Part of me was still angry. And I knew that part of me always would be. But I had chosen this. When I had first been welcomed into Billings, I had known what these girls were capable of, at least to some extent, and I had still chosen them because I knew what they could do for me. I knew the kind of future I could have with them. And in the here and now, they made me feel special. Important. Like I had true friends. In the end, that was what this whole game had been about. They might have had a sick way of going about it, but they'd just wanted to make sure that I was a true friend.

It was all about loyalty, just as Whittaker had said. Loyalty was paramount.

Lesson officially learned.

"So, are we okay?" Ariana asked finally.

"Yeah. Can we get back to the party already?" Noelle added, pushing herself up. "I'm very over this conversation."

"Yeah," I said, and almost couldn't believe I'd said it. "We're okay."

I was exhausted, crashing from my adrenaline rush, but somehow I managed to lift myself up off the bench. Taylor gave me a quick hug and slipped out ahead of us. Kiran kissed both my cheeks and winked, then followed. Ariana simply lifted the curtain and ducked out. I was about to go after her, when I realized that the most important question of the night had yet to be answered. I stopped and turned to face Noelle.

"So, those files I found on Ariana's computer—the crib sheets and the IMs," I said. "Those were planted too?"

Noelle smiled slowly. "Everything for a reason, remember, Reed? Everything for a reason."

Over

Hours later we emerged onto Park Avenue together, holding hands, laughing, trying to hold Kiran up as she fumbled and stumbled. The entire night had been a blur of drinks and dancing, of stories and sightings. I had avoided the alcoves for the rest of the night, sticking to the safety of the ballroom with the rest of the girls. Noelle and Dash had disappeared for an hour and came back looking disheveled and groggy and satisfied. Kiran had made off with a group of people from Kent and had returned to us in a different gown, which cracked everyone up. A personal joke I didn't quite get, but that I didn't ask about. I had a feeling that I didn't want to know.

Thanks to the white-gift tradition, Kiran had on a white fur stole over that new gown, Taylor was toting a gorgeous Chanel bag, Ariana had a pair of Dior shoes dangling from her fingers, and Noelle was wearing a crystal tiara that I knew would join the pile of junk under her bed the moment we got home. I had traded a seriously ugly designer belt with a girl from Barton to get the beautiful Tiffany white-gold-and-sapphire ring I now wore around the ring finger of my right hand. Other than Whittaker's diamonds, this was my first real jewelry ever. I couldn't help holding up my hand to admire it every five seconds.

I was doing just that when a beefy hand slipped into mine and the courtyard gate locked behind us. I looked up, startled and slightly tipsy, to find Whittaker hovering over me.

"Whit!" I said with a smile. "Where have you been?"

"That's exactly what I was going to ask you," he said a bit petulantly. "I barely saw you all night."

Behind me, Noelle, Ariana, and Taylor giggled, snorting their laughter through their noses.

"I know. I'm sorry," I said, laying a hand on his chest. "I was celebrating with my girls."

"Celebrating what?" he asked.

Noelle came up and threw her arm around Whittaker's large shoulders. "Girl stuff, baby. Girl. Stuff," she said, slapping his face on the last two words.

That sent her into drunken hysterics and I had to laugh along. Maybe I was a bit tipsier than I realized.

"Come on, you guys," Josh announced, trying to get the rabble in order. "We're going to miss the last train."

We followed after him, an unsteady mess of high heels and silk, unbuttoned shirts and lost jackets. Whittaker, who seemed mightily sober, kept his arm wrapped around me and I was grateful both for the warmth and the added stability. I could hear the girls' uneven footsteps behind me and knew it would be a miracle if no one broke an ankle.

"Did you at least have a good time?" he asked.

"Oh! The best!" I announced. "Thank you so much for letting me be your plus-one."

"You're quite welcome," he said, squeezing me a bit closer to him. "So, I was thinking, perhaps when the cold weather comes, we might take a trip out to my family's house in Tahoe. I'm sure my parents would love to meet you."

I tripped on a seam in the sidewalk and grabbed onto him to steady myself.

Parents. Meeting. Meeting the parents. No. Wrong. For a moment the world spun, but then it all clicked back into place. I pushed away from Whittaker slightly, standing on my own two feet, and tipped my head back to look at him.

"Whit? Can I talk to you for a second?" I asked. "Alone."

"Of course," he said. He looked at the others. "You can go ahead. We'll be right behind you."

Noelle shot me a knowing look, then walked off with the others in tow. I took a deep breath. Even in my tipsy state I knew what I had to do. This had gone on long enough. Whittaker deserved to know the truth.

"Whittaker, I'm really sorry, but I don't think we should see each other anymore."

"Excuse me?" Whittaker said.

"I'm sorry. I really like you. You're a great guy," I said. "But the truth is . . . I'm just not attracted to you."

"Oh," Whittaker said, looking at his shoes. "Well. That was blunt."

"I'm sorry! I didn't mean it to be," I said, my eyes swimming. "I just thought you'd appreciate the truth."

Whittaker took a deep breath and nodded. "I do," he said gamely. "I can't say I'm not disappointed, but I'm glad you were honest."

I tilted my head. "Aw, Whit. You are so gonna make some girl very happy one day."

Whittaker laughed. "I hope so," he said.

I teetered on my heels and he slipped his arm around my shoulders. I'd just broken up with him and he was still looking out for me, steadying me. It made me think of Constance and how she'd taken my hand during services that morning when they'd announced Thomas's disappearance. Suddenly, sadly, I hoped more than anything that those two would somehow get together. They were completely perfect for one another.

"You will!" I told him, my words slurring together. "In fact, I know someone. You know her, too. You just have to go out with her once and you'll totally fall in love with her."

Whittaker smiled wistfully. "Maybe we should talk about this on the train," he said, starting to walk and taking me along.

"Okay," I said, my eyes half-closing as we moved down the street.

The train, a soft seat, maybe a nap, sounded like a fabulous idea. But even as I looked forward to it, I couldn't believe that it was over. The Legacy, my "relationship" with Whit, my first trip to

NYC—it was all done. And it had all passed in a blur, with no sign of Thomas.

In the end, he had never shown. In the end, I hadn't even needed to be there. I took a deep breath and sighed grimly. Suddenly all I could think about was getting back to Easton and putting it all behind me.

getting a life

I rested my temple on the cool glass of the train's window and watched the world come to life as the sun slowly rose above autumn-colored trees. The hum of the train had long since swept most of my classmates off to slumber, but I couldn't tear my eyes off the view. It was too incredibly beautiful. Beautiful and blurred and ripe with possibility. I didn't want to miss anything.

All around me people snoozed and snored. Noelle had passed out with her head on Dash's shoulder, her tiara askew. His jacket had been pulled up to half cover his face and his arm rested around Noelle's back, his fingers curled around her elbow in a loving, gentle way. Every so often I glanced back at them and smiled. It was the most at peace they had ever been in my presence.

Somewhere in the back of the car, Ariana and Taylor whispered. Kiran was dead to the world, laid across a three-seater with her fur under her head on Gage's lap and Whittaker's jacket over her. Whit had attempted to get Gage to give her his coat, to which Gage had replied, "Yeah, right. I get cold, too, you know." So

Whittaker had immediately taken off his own jacket and spread it over Kiran's prone form. Now Whit dozed at the front of the car, hugging himself, snoring louder than anyone.

I heard a sigh and glanced left. Natasha sat up straight in the far window seat, her knee up, her elbow resting on it, holding her fingers to her mouth. She stared out at the world, pensive and sad, and I wondered what our relationship was going to be like now. She had shared her biggest secret with me, though admittedly not by choice. Would we be friends now? Remain enemies? I hoped it was the former. Now that I knew she wasn't an actual blackmailer, I had a feeling she might be interesting to get to know.

Someone stepped into my line of vision and I blinked out of a trance I hadn't realized I was in. I looked up slowly into Josh's face and my heart thumped. That was the second time tonight. What, exactly, was my heart up to?

"Hey," I said.

"Hey. Mind if I . . . ?" He gestured at the empty seat.

"No. Go ahead."

Josh sat down and blew out a sigh, pressing his palms into his thighs and settling back. Of all the guys on the train, he was the least disheveled. Shirt still tucked in, tie only slightly loosened, all but one button done. It didn't escape me that this meant he most likely had kept his hands to himself all night. Somehow, the realization of this made me happy.

"So. Interesting night, huh?" he said.

"Definitely. I would definitely say that," I replied.

"But . . . no Thomas."

The train hit a turn and squealed like mad. I caught my breath and pressed my fingers into the seat back in front of me. Josh chuckled and touched my arm.

"It's okay. Just a turn," he said.

"No. I know," I said.

What had freaked me out more was that I hadn't thought about Thomas once since I'd seen Leanne and Natasha together. I had forgotten all about him.

And maybe that was a good thing.

"I'm sure he's okay," I said. Mostly just to have something to say.

The truth was, at that very moment, I no longer cared. He had left me. He had bailed without the courtesy of a good-bye and left me there to fend for myself with the Billings Girls and Whittaker and the police. Clearly he didn't care about me. I had done everything I could, even dated a guy I wasn't remotely attracted to, in order to solidify my invite to the Legacy and the possibility of seeing him, but he hadn't even cared enough to show up. He had to have known there was a good chance I would be there, but he had stayed away.

No. As of that moment, I was over Thomas Pearson. As of that moment, I was moving on.

"Yeah. I'm sure he is," Josh said, sounding none too convinced.

"You know what? I don't want to talk about Thomas anymore,"

I said. "I mean, I want him to be okay and everything, but to tell you the truth, I'm over him. He's off having his life, and that's fine. But it also means that I get to have mine."

Josh glanced at me, eyebrows raised. "Really?"

"Really," I replied with a nod.

"That's very healthy of you," he said.

"I think so."

With that, I yawned hugely, feeling as if about a liter of my adrenaline had been drained right out of my body. My eyes drooped and I leaned over to rest my head on Josh's shoulder.

"Tired?" he asked.

"Yeah. Kind of."

"Here."

He lifted his arm and let me cuddle into him. My pulse raced at the intimacy of this gesture, but it also felt perfectly normal. Natural. If nothing else, Josh had been a good friend to me over the past few weeks, and now I found I was totally comfortable with him. More comfortable than I'd ever been with Whit. Certainly more comfortable than I'd ever been with Thomas, who constantly kept a girl guessing, both in good ways and bad.

I lasted about two seconds before my neck developed a strain. I moved my head around, trying to find a comfortable spot, and Josh lifted his arm again and nudged me, directing me down until my head was resting on his thigh.

Ah, yeah. That was comfort.

"Thanks," I murmured.

"Not at all," he replied.

As I started to drift off, listening to the hushed sounds of my friends' whispers, the lulling rhythm of the train, I could have sworn I felt Josh's fingertips slowly, gently, brushing my hair back behind my ear.

And I smiled.

so dead

By the time we got everyone off the train and trudged our way back through the streets of Easton proper, the last traces of dawn were fading away, leaving a nice, thick mist in their wake. High heels sank through the dewy grass into the soft earth, making it difficult to walk. Finally I just pulled them off, causing my feet to sigh in relief. I hooked the shoes over my fingers and wiggled my toes as I walked. The relief lasted about ten seconds. After that my feet were frigid blocks of ice.

"Are you okay?" Josh asked, bumping me lightly with his arm.

"Fine. Just can't wait to get home."

Home. Easton was home. Billings was home. It was the first time I'd realized that.

Eventually we arrived at the fence that surrounded Easton's grounds. We felt our way along the iron bars until we reached the craggy opening, hidden by evergreen bushes. Each of us ducked through, one by one, holding skirts to keep them from getting snagged, whispering directions so that no one bumped their heads. Now that we'd had the night of our lives, no one had bothered to change back into jeans and sweaters. If we got caught now, it would make no difference what we were wearing, and everyone had been too tired to change.

Once on the other side of the fence, I stuck close to Josh's side, not wanting to lose him in the fog. As we ascended the hill, I could hear the voices of the others but couldn't quite make them out.

"Eerie, huh?" Josh said.

I shivered and hugged my bare arms. "Yeah. But at least it might keep us from getting spotted."

If this party happened every year, if thirty kids traipsed back to school drunk and in party clothes every year at dawn, how they never got caught was a mystery. The closer we got to the classroom and dorm buildings, the more my teeth chattered and my bones shook. If we got caught, I was dead. If we got caught it would all have been all for nothing.

We cut across the soccer field and ducked along the tree line that would bring us up behind Billings and the other upperclassmen dorms. We paused en masse to catch our breath. There was no sound except the sound of our breathing. The fog muted everything.

"Everyone ready?" Dash whispered.

A few people nodded. I could hardly breathe. This was it. A few more moments and we'd be safe.

"Go!"

Everyone ducked and ran. Josh clutched my hand and a few

people laughed as we crossed the last few yards of open space between the tree line and the west wall of Dayton House, one of the girls' dorms. Once there, we all gathered against the cold, wet brick, gasping for air and counting our blessings. The mist was not so heavy here among the campus buildings. I was about to break away from Josh and head for Billings, when I looked around at my friends and realized that all of their faces were flashing red, then blue, then red, then blue.

"What *is* that?" someone said.

"Hang on."

Josh disentangled his hand from mine and crept to the corner of the building. At first he simply peeked his head around, but then his shoulders slumped and he stepped right out into the open.

"Oh, my God," he said.

All the air whooshed out of me. "What?"

Not even the fear of being caught could have stopped us from satisfying our curiosity. We all moved carefully to the corner and gathered around Josh. What I saw made me want to sink to my knees and turn and run all at once.

Police cars. Everywhere. On the grass between the dorms. In the quad. Every student in school was outside their dorms in various stages of dress, whispering and looking around as cops in uniforms circled among them, talking in low tones or shouting orders.

"We are so dead," someone behind me said.

I had to agree. Clearly every police officer within a hundred-mile radius had been called to the scene. And why not? Thirty students missing? Thirty of the most precious and overprivileged sons and daughters in the country? Of course the authorities would respond in droves.

"No. It's not for us," Josh said. "Look at them."

So I did. And he was right. Some of the students sat on the benches, wide-eyed and open mouthed. Others cried. Three girls hugged one another over near the back entrance of Bradwell. Somewhere nearby someone was clearly sobbing.

"What the hell is going on?" Dash said.

"Let's go."

With that, Dash, Gage, Josh, and Whittaker, along with a few other guys, jogged ahead. The rest of us were rooted to the spot. There was only one word in my mind.

"Thomas," I whispered.

I whirled around and looked at Noelle. Her skin was as white as the mist swirling all around her. She stared past me, unblinking.

"Do you think it's—"

Pounding footsteps interrupted my words. A hand fell on my shoulder. Instantly every pore in my body filled with dread.

"Reed," Josh said, his voice harsh and strained. "Reed."

I turned around slowly. I didn't want to look at him. Didn't want to see on his face what I had already heard in his voice. He stood before me, panting. Anguished tears streamed down his face.

"It's Thomas. They found his body," he said, bracing his

hands over his knees. "Reed, he's . . . Thomas is dead."

I shut my eyes and squeezed my hands into fists, so tight I could feel my nails breaking through the skin of my palms. I silently begged my heart to keep on beating. I willed my lungs to keep filling with air. I looked down at my hands, at my new ring glittering in the flashing lights. I tried to concentrate on this. And only this.

I knew if I opened my mouth even the tiniest crack I would start screaming. I would just start screaming and I would never, ever be able to stop.

You're invited to a sneak peek of
the next book in the Private series:

untouchable

decision

Ninety percent out of it and I was still learning things. For instance:

The curious stares of your peers become pretty easy to ignore when you're working on approximately forty-five minutes of sleep spread out over three days. Also, the cafeteria manager doesn't like it when he finds someone sitting on the cold brick outside the door waiting for him to unlock it. Cheerios expand when left to soak in milk for too long. If you spend enough time gazing blankly at them, you can watch it happen.

A few days had passed since Thomas's funeral and still I had hardly eaten or slept. The area under my eyes felt full and tight and heavy at all times, like I could either pass out or burst into tears at any second. The door to the cafeteria opened and I looked up from my Cheerios instinctively, an image of Thomas flashing through my mind. A queasy warmth hit me and I felt like so wretchedly stupid I wanted to scream. It wasn't Thomas. It was never going to be Thomas. Figure it out, Reed.

"Are you all right?"

Somehow I lifted my eighty-pound head and looked up at Josh. He hovered at the end of the otherwise deserted cafeteria table with a tray full of doughnuts and chocolate milk. Boy took in more sugar before nine a.m. than most five-year-olds did in a day.

"M'fine," I mumbled. "Just wishing this bowl was a pillow."

I pushed my tray aside and rested my elbows on the table, taking a long, deep breath to try to crowd out the nausea. Josh sat down across from me and lifted his messenger bag over his head, placing it on the floor. He wore a blue and yellow rugby shirt with a green paint stain on one of the yellow stripes. His curls were sticking out adorably in all directions.

Adorably. I wanted to flog myself. Thomas was dead. I was not supposed to be noticing that other guys were adorable.

Under the table, Josh fumbled with his bag. He slapped his hand to his mouth, then took a chug of his chocolate milk to help him swallow.

"What was that?" I asked.

"Vitamins," Josh said. "One a day keeps the doctor away."

"You are a parent's wet dream," I told him.

"Tell that to my parents," he said.

I smiled. It was nice that he could make me smile even in my current state of semi-consciousness.

Josh lowered his body toward the table a bit, in confab mode. I leaned in as well. "So, I've thought about it, and I've decided to go to the cops like Noelle said," he whispered.

He bit into a powdered doughnut and sugar sprayed everywhere. I looked at him and wondered if I was dreaming. Did he really just tell me that he was going to rat out Thomas, and then take a big old bite of doughnut? I couldn't even swallow one spoonful of cereal this morning and he seemed, well, fine. In fact, for the past few days, Josh had been keeping it together better than anyone else I knew, which made little to no sense. Thomas was his roommate. His friend. And I hadn't even seen him cry once. But what did I know? Maybe he went back to his room and blubbered in private all night long. It wouldn't be the first time someone around Easton kept a secret.

"You really think that's necessary?" I asked.

"Noelle was right," Josh said, chewing. "That guy she was talking about? Rick? He was Thomas's local supplier and he's a total wackjob. I would bet money he had something to do with this."

I took a deep breath, straightened my back for a second, then slumped again. "I don't know, Josh. Do we really want Thomas's parents to know all this stuff? I know he was into some scary crap, but he was trying to change. Did he tell you he was on his way to rehab the night he left?"

Josh blurted out a laugh and took a sip of milk, smiling in mirth. I suddenly felt very hot all over.

"What?" I said.

Josh blinked at me and then his face fell. "Oh. You're serious," he said.

"Yes, I'm serious," I said, beyond offended.

Josh put his milk down and wiped his hands on his jeans. "Reed, I hate to be the one to tell you this, but Thomas was the last person who was ever going to rehab. He was so wasted the last night he was here you could have wrung him out and served shots."

The cafeteria had just become a Gravitron, whirling and tilting and heading for the sky. There was no way to focus, so I closed my eyes.

"What?" I said, my mouth dry.

"I came back from the library and he was on the phone screaming at Rick, so gone he couldn't even stand up straight," Josh whispered. "That's why I think Noelle might be right. Thomas was pretty livid and I bet he said some stuff he wouldn't have said if he wasn't such a mess. I didn't think much of it at the time, because those two were always at each other's throats over something, but maybe this time he really pissed Rick off somehow."

I pressed the heel of my hand into my forehead, trying to make sense of all of this. Thomas was drunk? But that morning he had been so sincere about quitting. And he'd left me that note. He was going to some holistic treatment center. He was getting help.

Had that all been a lie?

"This doesn't make any sense," I said aloud.

"What?" Josh asked.

Wait a minute, wait a minute. Why would he leave me that note if he wasn't actually planning on leaving? I would have been kind of suspicious if I had found the note that night and then seen him on campus the next day. So he must have been planning on going somewhere. But where?

"Maybe it was just a last hurrah," I suggested. "Maybe he wanted to get drunk one last time before going to rehab?"

It sounded totally pathetic even as I said it. So pathetic that Josh actually had pity in his eyes.

"Reed, what makes you so sure that Thomas was going to rehab?" he asked gently.

The double doors opened and sunlight poured in. Noelle, Ariana, Taylor, and Kiran strode through and headed straight for the breakfast line. I didn't want them to hear any of this and start speculating. We had to talk fast.

"He left me a note," I confessed quickly. "I found it in one of my books. He said he was going to a treatment center and not to try to find him. He said he was leaving that night."

Josh laughed derisively and shook his head. "Leave it to Pearson. I bet the last words out of his mouth were a lie."

A thump of dread warmed my insides. "What do you mean?"

Josh looked at me as if he'd just realized who he was talking to. "Nothing. Forget it," he said.

"Josh—"

"It's just . . ." He crumpled a napkin and squeezed it in his fist. "I just don't think that Thomas ever fully appreciated what he had when he had you, that's all."

My mouth fell open slightly and I snapped it closed. Josh stared at me intently. No averted eyes, no quick change of subject. He really meant what he had just said. I was both flattered and completely thrown. He'd just implied that Thomas had lied to me nonstop . . . and complimented me in the same breath.

"Reed, you have to show that note to the police," Josh said.

"How do you know I haven't?" I asked.

"Have you?"

"No," I admitted miserably.

"It's evidence," Josh said. "It might be the last thing Thomas ever wrote. They need to see it."

My stomach felt acidic and warm. I had been dreading this

moment for weeks, but Josh was right. When he put it that simply, it seemed obvious. Besides, I had only kept the note a secret to protect Thomas from his parents hunting him down. Now that was no longer an issue.

"You're right," I said, determined. "I'll go right after morning services."

Just thinking about it made me feel monumentally better. I was nervous to let the police know I had hidden something from them, but I couldn't wait to be free of it. Thomas had lied to me. Who knew how often or about what? It was no longer my responsibility to protect him. It was about time I got this whole thing over with, once and for all.

private

KATE BRIAN

Welcome to Easton Academy, where secrets and lies are all part of the curriculum . . .

Fifteen-year-old Reed Brennan is delighted when she wins a scholarship to Easton Academy – it's the golden ticket out of her suburban life and away from her pill-popping mother. But when she arrives at the beautiful, tradition-steeped campus, everyone is more sophisticated, more gorgeous and a WHOLE lot wealthier than she is.

Reed may have been accepted to the Academy, but she certainly hasn't been accepted by her classmates. She feels like she's on the outside, looking in . . . until she meets the Billings Girls.

They're the most beautiful, intelligent and powerful girls on campus. And, boy, do they know it. Reed vows to do whatever it takes to be accepted into their inner circle. But once she's in, she discovers much more than designer clothes hiding in their closets – there are also plenty of skeletons . . .

Secrets which must be kept PRIVATE. Whatever the cost.